They Told Me I Had To Write This

Kim Miller grew up freewheeling the back streets of country NSW where wheels meant freedom. Life changed when he went to live in a boys' home as a teenager. Following high school he was into motorbike dirt racing and ignoring university lectures. Somehow he made it to marriage and family. Kim works with people in and out of prison, managing a project called Home For Good in Newcastle, NSW. He still rides motorbikes and knows a bit about freedom.

Also by Kim Miller
Insiders

They Told Me I Had To Write This

Kim Miller

FORD ST

First published by Ford Street Publishing, an imprint of
Hybrid Publishers, PO Box 52, Ormond VIC 3204

Melbourne Victoria Australia

First published 2009
National Library of Australia
Cataloguing-in-Publication entry

Author: Miller, Kim 1949–
Title: They told me I had to write this /
Kim Miller

ISBN: 9781876462840 (pbk.)
Dewey Number: A823.4

Cover design: Grant Gittus Graphics
Artist: Michael Hardman

In-house editor: Saralinda Turner

Printed in Australia by McPherson's Printing Group

To Sam with love

TUESDAY, MARCH 3
THE REV

They told me I had to write this. It's taken a while to get started but here I am.

'Here I am.' Sounds like I'm talking to the coppers again.

'Here I am. Yes, sir. No, sir. OK I did it, sir. Here I am.'

The stuff I've been given up for. I can't believe it. People are still on my back in this place. Same old story. So here I am writing. Figure that one out.

Anyway, there's too many dead people in my world and I'm sick of being blamed. Being blamed for someone being dead sucks. Such is life. Ned Kelly said that. Saw a few people dead then wrote some letter and got famous. Brothers, Ned and me.

Don't count on this being a long letter. It's taken a while to get started but it's coz of what they told me. Well, anyway, the Rev told me and he's like the boss around here. The boss of Rocky Valley. The school for kids too hot to handle. You can spot the Rev because of the red-hot car and motorbike. He's a full-on Mr Revhead.

The car is old but serious. Falcon GT with the air scoop poking up through the bonnet. That air scoop comes alive with the motor and we call it the Shaker. We all want a ride, but guess what. He never gives anyone a lift. Not even if someone's missed the bus. Miss the bus and he'll just drive off. Leaving kids behind sucks.

His fancy motorbike's a one player game with no room for a passenger anyway. It's got this stupid lid where the back seat should be but it's for a toolkit or something. I reckon he should have a back seat coz that bike could take two people easy. Aprilia RSV1000R. Red and black like the Shaker and designed like it came from outer space.

You know what's twice stupid about his bike? It's got no seat for a passenger but it's got the foot-pegs. Too right. Foot-pegs, no seat, double stupid.

So that's it for Mr Revhead. And if he gets to see this he should take my advice about getting a back seat so he can take a passenger. Not that I want to go passenger with some teacher. Had that way back. They could have called him pedals, that other bloke. That rock spider. I'm not going there no more. No way am I.

But that Aprilia sure is a pretty bike. The Rev told me I had to write this. So here I am and now he can get off my back. It took me a long time to get going, but you probably already know that.

Do you? Do you know that stuff? I don't

know how it works, that kind of thing. But I'm your grandson and I know you still love me. There, I've said it.

Clem.

WEDNESDAY, MARCH 11
COPPING THE COPPERS

Dear Gram

The coppers were here again. At school I mean. This time it was worse than when they were after Bundy.

His name isn't Bundy it's Barry, but his hair is almost white, even his eyebrows. His chin is seriously fuzzy like he should get to his dad's shaver and he's like a polar bear so he gets everyone to call him Bundy. He's pretty big so we call him that. Hey, you've got to choose your battles carefully around here.

The first time the coppers came I got off the bus real careful and slid out of the way quiet as. My heart was beating like it was about to give me up no matter what. The coppers were here for Troy's broken arm, which Bundy had done. We didn't know it was broken but his mum took him to hospital and then somebody called the coppers.

That's how it is with some of the fights around here. Had some bruises but no broken arms or anything. Bundy reckons he's hot property with the coppers after him, but the story from Troy was that he did his arm falling off his bike. Anyway, the nurse figured Troy should have some gravel rash and his mum got a bit suss. His mum gets suss and we get the coppers. Mostly I try to stay out of Bundy's way. I'm learning.

Anyway, this morning on my bike I saw the coppers and took off on autopilot. Then I thought, can't be anything they want me for or they would get me at home. Cooled down and rode back to school. Then had to say why I was late. Bit close there for a while but not like it was last year.

Having coppers close up gets me going but this school has a secret weapon for guys like Bundy, which is Mr Sykes. If you put Bundy between a couple of weightlifters and roll them into one you end up with Mr Sykes. He takes no prisoners and Bundy slows up something noticeable around Mr Sykes.

But this letter has gone on long enough.

Clem.

MONDAY, MARCH 16
TXT

Dear Gram

U R 2 KEWL! Dad reckons I run up too

much money on texting. Of course he'd say that. Here's another one, U R Gr8 Xlnt C U L8r.

This boy Peter can text as fast as we can write. One of the teachers calls him Repeater coz he's so fast. Get it? We just call him Pete. He's a bit like me and doesn't like being called by his full name. His mum is always 'Peter this – Peter that'. I guess that's the way mothers do it.

Who ever heard of anyone being called Clement? I prefer Clem. Some of the boys call me Clam coz I never say much. I don't like Clam either.

Parents should be careful with kids' names but being a Dylan is very brilliant. Clem Dylan is all up cool for a name. Another plus for Dylan is a song by this dude Bob Dylan that we did in class. The song is like,

Fathers throughout the land.

Don't criticise

You don't understand

Your sons are beyond your command.*

I have made it a rap song here because the original needed help, but that song is so true about my dad.

Discussion on that song was pretty hot I can tell you. It says something about fathers which is Velcro between me and Bob Dylan. That shows you what names can do.

Another boy here is Jackson but he wants

us to call him Jacko coz he's whacko. His mum calls him Jackson and he rolls his eyes like, 'Who ever calls me Jackson?' But one day I heard her call him Jacko as he got in the car and he went seriously off at her. 'Call me Jackson,' he yelled.

What's that about? Her one thing and us another thing. Weird. Didn't ask him about it, but. He's got this t-shirt, 'My mum went to the $2 Shop and all I got was this lousy t-shirt'. Should be happy he's even got a mum I reckon.

I'm gonna finish coz this letter suddenly stings me.

Clem.

FRIDAY, MARCH 20
A WAY OUT? DON'T COUNT ON IT.

Dear Gram

Life goes on at Rocky Valley and we're all getting out on the bike track. We're in the bush a bit and there's the maddest track up behind the school. It's a proper bush racing track and long distance. There's about twenty k of tracks and you can do short loops or the whole thing.

Some of it is deadly steep, like off a cliff. I don't know why they made it so steep. It's not like there's anything up there or anything, just gnarly old washouts.

One steep bit follows this gully and when

it rains the whole thing is a slippery mess like riding up a creek. We all reckon it's dangerous but they still make us do races on it, even downhill. If we want to we can take another track but it takes longer that way and most of the kids do that, but then they never win that section. It's even got a sign saying The Way Out. It's not, but. Not the way out. It's just another way to the same place. At the other end you're still there, still riding, still pushing like mad past all the mud and rocks and stuff.

Take The Way Out and someone with a bit of skill on the gully track gets ahead of you. I've seen the Rev do that. Get ahead of anyone, he can, up the gully or down. You should see him on a mountain bike. It's as if he's on his superhot Aprilia. I don't know how he does it, ride the gully like that I mean. Must be some secret.

His mountain bike is not red and black like the Aprilia; it's a Bianchi and it's kind of silver, kind of blue. Looks magic with that tucked away shock in back. That's what I want one day, decent shockers. Aprilia and Bianchi. Those Italians sure know how to put a bike together.

Clem.

FRIDAY, MARCH 27

Dear Gram

I've been a while coz we've been camping in the bush. We go camping a lot and that is mostly excellent, but not this week. This camp was a two-day thing and it rained. I reckon they must have known it was going to rain. How can somebody mess that up with the TV telling you anyway?

So we walked there in the rain and we walked out in the rain. When we got back to the school Dad was there to pick me up. Mostly I ride or get the bus. My dad can tell when it's raining, must be improving.

Clem.

MONDAY, MARCH 30

Dear Gram

The coppers were at school again this morning. I didn't go off like I used to but it was weird riding past that cop car as if I didn't care. Turns out to be only one copper and he was setting up some bike races with the PCYC kids from town. RVS against PCYC. Let's see who gets most up the nose of the others that day. Can't wait.

Anyway having that cop car there was a bit like an omen coz it wasn't long before I was in trouble anyway and the trouble was about me not saying much which is full-on unfair if you think about it.

We were in the paddock doing agriculture with Mr Sykes and I was staying quiet because of the coppers when somebody made a comment about my name. Mostly I let this stuff pass and get the guy later. But today when somebody said the unfunny Clem the Clam joke, this smart-arse named Brian said, 'Clem is a man of few words and one day he will learn the meaning of both of them.' I went right off and said, 'Well here's the meaning of them both. One in this hand and one in the other.'

Then I was into him with my fists like you wouldn't believe. But Mr Sykes is like a mountain and he grabbed us both before I could really get going and suddenly my fists weren't much use to me.

But what is really weird is that Mr Sykes got Brian to apologise, which was OK by me, but then he got me to apologise which was not so easy coz Brian is a full-on headache and a bit of bruising would shut him up. Shut him up. Ha, that's funny, coz we sometimes call him 'windows'. Well, his name's Dawson, don't blame me. Anyway, part of the landscape at

Rocky Valley is Mr Sykes getting in the way more often than is helpful.

So the coppers set me up for a bad day but I am hoping that things settle down a bit where the cops are concerned, and at least it was Brian and not Bundy. This place is full of people who set me off, but this is the first time Mr Sykes has had to get hold of me like that. I don't know if that is bad or good but at least the day is over.

Love,

Clem.

THURSDAY, APRIL 2
REV REVISITED

Dear Gram

Did I tell you that I see the Rev every week or two? Well I do. All the kids here have a teacher that they see like this for a private talk. It's OK but it can get a bit hectic. If it gets like that I go and look out the window to the car park. I check out the Aprilia or the Shaker and my mind goes somewhere silent in amongst the red and the black.

Mostly I try to stay private but when I'm talking with the Rev sometimes things slip out, like the time I said something about that teacher in year five. I shut up pretty quick when that came out. The Rev doesn't bag me out or put me down or anything. Didn't even mention the fight with Brian which was a surprise to me.

Sometimes it's as if he knows what I mean even before I say it. And even when he's ahead of me he doesn't shut me down. My old teachers never let me finish, but this place is different and the Rev is OK.

This week I was telling him about some of the trouble I had in primary school with getting sent home all the time for losing it and going fully sick at that teacher when he said things about me in front of the other kids.

Trouble is, talking with the Rev can get me upset and I feel such a loser. Like I was back then. Even writing about it sets me off.

I hate it when this happens.

Clem.

FRIDAY, APRIL 8

Dear Gram

'Do you remember where we finished last time?' That's how the Rev starts off in session. Do I ever? One sentence from him and my heart starts racing. But this time I'm going to stick it out.

Well, I will try to tell you the rest of our session coz it got so I was about ready to start crying before and that was pretty terrible coz it made me feel like some emo loser. At least the Rev didn't say what it looked like from his point of view and it got so I could tell him about how Dad never listened to me about that teacher back in primary school.

Why didn't Dad listen to me back then? That's what I want to know. Even to talk about it here makes me want to get Dad's neck in one hand and a blunt instrument in the other. Just like back then. But you can't do that when you are only ten years old.

The Rev must have been shocked when I told him how I used to feel back then.

Well I don't mind giving the Rev a bit of a shocker coz it was me that lived through it all and I was only a kid and it's no wonder the teachers had to send me home so much and not even Dad would believe me when I told him about that teacher doing that weird stuff. Anyway, he should be in jail for doing that to a little kid. Why don't they put guys like that in jail, Gram?

I'm going to stop, even if the Rev does think all this writing stuff is so important.

Love from

Clem.

DvD Review in 100 words

'Oliver Twist'

Mr & Mrs Hartley showed this DvD at the Shack called Oliver Twist. It was a black and white DvD and more than a bit old. It's about this boy in a terrible orphanage in London and he gets into trouble with the coppers. Some people say they'll help him but they only get him into more trouble. The bad guy's name is Bill Sykes, the same name as our ag teacher, but he ends up dead.

TUESDAY, APRIL 7
THIS IS THE HARD BIT

Dear Gram

The Rev has a real name. It's Mr Paterson. That is Latin for being his father's son. Well who else's son could he be? You can't be someone else's son except your own father's can you? And your mother's of course, but that doesn't apply here.

Why did she die, Gram? I couldn't tell the Rev what happened coz I don't know. When we were talking this week I just started telling him but there was nothing much to tell, just that I never knew her coz she died when I was being born in the first place.

The Rev said, 'Have you ever asked other family members about her?'

I said, 'There aren't many other family members, just Dad and Gram.'

And that made me think it must have been tough on you for all this time with me around. But you always wanted me to be at your place and Dad seemed never to want me much at all.

Well, that's the way it seemed to me this week when I was talking with the Rev. He sure gets under your skin.

Anyway, it makes me feel bad but I'm not going to let it stop me writing to you this time.

Instead I'll tell you about Jason and Pete. Jason is another kid from school and Pete is the super-fast texter. Well, they are cousins and grew up living with their grandma, just like you and me when Dad was away. Wish I had a cousin who could have lived at your place. Brilliant. Like having a brother.

Jason and Pete are not the same age but they are in the same class coz one of them repeated when he was little, just like I did. I don't know which one, but wouldn't it be funny if it was Pete who repeated?

So, there you go, something funny even when I was feeling so poisonous about that stuff in primary school.

Holidays coming up. Mr Hartley is doing bike stuff for anyone who wants to. I'm aiming to get some gully practice.

Till then,

Clem.

SATURDAY, APRIL 25
STOKIN'

Dear Gram

I've been out on the bike track for most of the holidays. Lots of the kids from school have been the same. Mr Hartley takes us into the mountains or we do track training. In this school even the teachers go mountain bike racing with us.

I've got the gully sorted I reckon. I can go up pretty easily. Don't get scared by it any more, but I'm a bit nervous about coming down. That is seriously megatastic. Jason and Pete think it's fully sick. Uphill is easier for me coz I'm skinny but some of the other boys are seriously unskinny. They need to get out on the bikes more.

My own bike is better than the school bikes but it's still only a hardtail. I've asked Dad to get me one with proper shockers. That would be totally wicked. Mostly he puts me off but I think the school is starting to get through to him a bit and he's not so off when I ask him about it these days.

Having full shockers on that gully would get me wired and no one could catch me I reckon. Perhaps the Rev and Mr Sykes. They are the most out there of the teachers in the bush. I reckon we should swap bikes. That would be serious traffic.

Your stokin' grandson.

Clem.

Dear Gram

Back to school, which really means back to classes coz I've been here so much through the holidays.

Did I tell you that we get to do our School Certificate here? Well we do, even though it's not like my old school. They didn't tell us that when we started. They didn't tell us much of anything, they just moved us here. Thought it was only me but we all started the same.

Finish here well enough and it's back to normal school with the School Certificate. If they saw my reports from the other schools they wouldn't say that.

I reckon you'd like the idea of me getting my School Certificate. You were always telling me how important it was to get things like that, I can remember you saying lots of things like that before you . . .

Now I'm starting to cry even. I hate all this. All I want to do is to be normal with a dad and a mum and a gram.

You said lots of things about me getting on in school before you got so sick.

Before you died.

Now I've done it. I've said it.

The Rev wondered if I could get to here and

keep writing. Well I showed him up on that one, the old Rev, coz I'm still going full on.

Gram, did you really get sick because of me? Dad reckons you did. Well that's what he said one time, and pretty loud that night. But he was angry at me and had a lot of beer in him. Anyway, he reckons it was me that made you sick coz I was such a worry to you.

Was it, Gram?

This is a pass or fail question here. Was it me?

Clem.

Mrs H Talks Food

Mrs Hartley is a mean cook of chops when it comes to that steel plate on the fire at the Shack. Somebody asked, 'How long should you leave chops on the BBQ?' Mrs H said, 'It's not something you do by the clock. It's knowing when they don't need any more heat.' It's about time my dad took the heat off me.

THURSDAY, APRIL 12
A QUESTION THAT WON'T GO AWAY

Dear Gram

I don't know how life and death and everything works but I hope you can read this. When I was writing last time I didn't mean that I thought what Dad was saying was right or anything. But is it? Can one person make somebody else sick like that?

And what about my mum?

I mean, how could I have made anyone sick when I was just being born? That's what I want to know. Not even the Rev would know that I reckon. Not Mr Sykes or Jason or Pete or anybody. But you might know.

I've got to know this, Gram. Dad reckons it was me that made Mum die and it was me that made you get sick and die. How can he know that? Forever he's been telling me that I made Mum die, forever, even before I was at school he's reckoned that it was me. What if it's true?

What about that day in the bike shop when he almost bought my bike? That mate from school came in with his mum and they started looking at bikes and Dad said, 'Let's get out of here.' It was weeks before we went back for my bike. That boy being in the bike shop with his mum was not my fault.

Do you reckon I should tell him that I've been writing to you? He might get really mad at me again and it's been ages since that happened.

I reckon the Rev should have to say what he thinks on this. He doesn't say much about what he thinks. Just waits for me to say stuff. He's never said that it was my fault about Mum and you. Never. I wish Dad was like that.

Wish you were here,

Clem.

FRIDAY, MAY 1
THE QUESTION AND DAD

Dear Gram

I thought about asking Dad why he reckons it was my fault. I've thought about it lots of times but when I'm with him I get too scared to ask. I guess I'm still chicken-hearted on these things. I don't want to be, I just am.

Anyway, he's got too much on his mind to ask about serious stuff at the moment. There's this new girlfriend. Her name's Lyndal. Too much like Mum's name for me.

So there's this new girlfriend. Except she's not a girl she's a woman. There's a difference. Anyway, they never last. They end up leaving or he drops them, or they fight until there's nothing left to hang on to and they fall apart like leaves from a tree, kind of shriveled.

I don't know if I want this one to last any longer. I used to think I wanted a mum so bad that Dad should just find someone for me, but his girlfriends aren't mum material. I can see that now but when I was little I never saw it. Just as well I had you all those years when Dad kept going away.

I'd like to have a girlfriend. Pete has a girlfriend. Some of the boys talk about girls but I reckon they make most of it up. With Pete it's different. He doesn't puff up about it like the others, keeps quiet mostly, so I guess I believe him.

Lyndal works where Dad works. What if they see each other at work and then after work and he brings her home? Then they might get sick of each other. I reckon you could get sick of the same person all the time and having to be nice to them all day.

What was it like for you and Granddad?

Clem.

WEDNESDAY, MAY 6
THE REV SHAKES ME UP

Dear Gram

I saw the Rev in town. He was in the Shaker. Remember the Shaker? There was his wife up front and three kids in the back seat. They were younger than me and I suppose that's his family. It was like the Rev and all the little revs, the revlets. Ha ha. They were all laughing at something and he didn't see me coz I was just coming out of a shop when they drove past. It was the first time I ever saw anyone in the car with him.

The Rev and I had our session yesterday. I told him I saw him with those people in the car and he didn't even tell me who they were. I was like – I saw you in town with the car full yesterday.

And he was like – Yeah, I was there all right.

And I was like – Were they your kids?

And he said – My family, you mean?

Yeah, your family.

He asked me – How did it appear to you, me with all those people?

I told him it looked like your wife and your kids.

He said – Tell me what you were thinking when you saw us all drive past.

And that's when I lost it.

How does he do that? I hate this stuff. I hate the crying and being lonely and I hate myself for what I did to you and to Mum. And I hate Dad for not believing me about that teacher. And I hate this school. I hate wanting to stop writing to you and I'm going to keep on writing even when I hate everything so much.

I don't always lose it but sometimes he makes me so angry that I explode right there in his office. That bloke gets under my skin and I never know when it's coming.

After I cooled down the Rev asked me again what I was thinking when I saw them in the car and I told him that it made me feel lonely. And that's the truth except for you.

I told him that I lived with you when Dad was away and he'd come back and I'd have to go to his house and he would yell at me and I learned to wait until he was going away again so I could move back in with you.

Until you got so sick. Since then Dad's had to put up with me on his own. Now I'm at this school he doesn't have to see me some nights coz of the live-ins and the camps so I guess we're getting on better because of that.

I managed to tell the Rev all that without losing it again. I feel OK about being able to do that. Mostly I can't get that far before I choke up again so I must be learning something.

I hope I don't see the Rev with his kids again for a long while.

Maybe I need to keep out of town and spend more time on the bike in the hills. I'm sure stokin' it at the moment on that track, makes me feel so fully righteous out there.

Your Favorite Grandson,

Clem.

WEDNESDAY, MAY 15
THE GULLY GETS UNDER MY SKIN

Dear Gram

I've been out riding the bike so I don't have to be in town as much. Seeing the Rev with those kids really set me off. 'Cept he never told me who they were. What if it was his sister with her kids, or neighbours or somebody? I never thought about that. I just went over the top in session coz of what was inside me. He must have thought I was a complete jerk. Well, he must have thought something when he saw me lose it.

Anyway, that's some of the stuff I've been thinking about while I've been out riding. That's the good thing about knowing the track so well, I can think about stuff while I still keep my eye on the track. Course I can't do it when I'm coming down the gully. And that's another thing I've learned.

I was riding down the gully and my mind went somewhere else and I spilled big time. I've got all this gravel rash down my side, legs, elbow, shoulder. The other guys love it when somebody spills and so I was up and running for the bike before anyone could pass on the news. The bike must have gone twenty metres down the hill before it stopped and I am full-on glad I didn't.

Till my gravel rash heals up I'm sticking to the smoother tracks and fire trails through the national park. We're allowed in there on mountain bikes but no motorbikes or anything, and especially no four-wheel-drives. I think that's OK, but the fourby people probably think it sucks. Anyway, it would be good to have a fourby to take our gear out on camps.

We had group this week with Mr O'Neill. We can call him Mike when we are out on camp, but we have to call him Mr O'Neill when we are in school, even at lunch and times like that. He does most of the small group sessions. I'm in a group with Hamish and Pete and Jacko and Brian. Sometimes we call him Brian the Brain coz he's got all the answers, but not all the right ones. Ha ha. Just that he thinks they're the right ones. This is the kind of kid that if he ever has a bright idea the lights in the room will dim coz of the amount of power it will require. We watch what we say to him coz he can be fully deadly, like when I reckoned his ears were only painted on. I sure learned from that one.

Anyway, Mr O'Neill was talking to us about three different ways of living in our own little world. There are people who are visuals, who mostly see the world through their eyes, and there are auditory people who hear their world through their ears, and there are kinner-somethings who feel the stuff in their world and I will remember that word properly someday you can count on that. And the visual people say things like, 'I see what you are getting at,' and the auditory people say things like, 'I hear what you are saying,' and the kinner-somethings say, 'I get a feel for what is happening here.'

So we're trying to check out what stuff we mostly say in group coz another boy will understand us better if we use words to suit the other person's style rather than our own, if you get what I mean.

Mr O'Neill knows this stuff backwards and he knows what we are and he says he's known it from the first session. He reckons he can tell what we are by looking at us when we are talking about stuff. How about that? It's how our eyes move. OK, it's weird but that's what he said. And we reckon I am a kinesthetic and I have remembered the word this time.

Anyway, he looks at Jacko and says, 'Jacko I can see that you are a visual, and seeing is an important way for you to learn about the world and you probably say things like, 'Yeah, I see what you mean.'

Well, Jacko went right off. He started on

about people looking at him all the time and they didn't have a right and suddenly he was talking about this guy in the Little Nippers in the surf lifesaving. So there he was going on about this coach in Little Nippers and, 'Look what he did back then,' and this coach was taking photos of all the kids without their Speedos on and showing them around the internet and the coppers caught this bloke and even Jacko's mum saw the photos they had of him coz she was in the court as a witness.

He was a fully sick peddo that guy I reckon and Jacko was crying in group and everything. That sucks, Gram. Sometimes I cry in private session but not in group, nobody ever does that. That would make everyone think 'Hardcore Emo!!' And that guy is now in jail coz he had so many photos of the Little Nippers like that and he did that for years before the coppers got him. And Jacko is now here coz of getting into so much trouble in normal school like I used to.

The funny thing is that Jacko is always up in front of people so they have to look at him. He's funny, that's why we call him Whacko Jacko, and he doesn't mind that, as long as it's one of his mates. He can get the teachers stirred up over something that he does and sometimes you can see the teachers trying not to smile when they tell him to cool it.

Poor Jacko. Always being in front of people with his funny stuff but he hates it when people look at him. All Mr O'Neill did was say that Jacko was a visual. Sure took everyone by surprise, that did.

Anyway, when he went fully off like that all us others just sat there and we didn't know how to handle it. And Mr O'Neill waited for Jacko to calm down and said that he could see that Jacko had been carrying some heavy stuff for a long time.

That's all he said and nobody else said anything. I reckon Mr O'Neill should have said something more than that to make Jacko feel better. Even when I'm telling you about him I can feel my eyes getting hot, for Jacko that is, but I won't let that happen coz there's more I want to say.

Do you remember what used to happen when I was living at your place and sometimes I fell off my bike or my razor scooter and mashed up my knees? I would get upset and crying and you would hold me like it was part hug and part hold-me-down until I stopped crying a bit so you could fix my knees. There was sand and dirt under the skin and you used to slowly get it out with that stuff and the washcloth.

Well, I reckon this school is a bit like that. It's a bit like being in one of your hold-me-downs while they get stuff out from under your skin. That's what I've been thinking about since Jacko got upset and it started me again on remembering that teacher in year five and that is why I wanted to cry for Jacko. If ever I have a son I'm never going to let that sort of stuff happen to him, no way.

So that's been my week and how I've got through it. Bit rough but it's over.

Your kinesthetic grandson, still feeling every bump since spilling in the gully.

Clem.

DvD Review in 100 words
'Lord of the Flies'

These kids crash in an aeroplane
on a desert island. The two
biggest boys start gangs and
two kids even get killed. There
is nothing about flies in the
DvD and it's also black and
white and pretty old. Some of
those kids haven't even got
any clothes left and I don't
reckon they should have movies
like that. Lucky for Ralph
the navy rescues him just as
the other gang is burning the
whole island down.

FRIDAY, MAY 15
NEVER LET A CHAINSAW KNOW YOU ARE IN A HURRY

Dear Gram

I reckon it's about time that I told you we do more here than just riding mountain bikes.

We do English and our English teacher is, get this one, Mr German. How about that? That is stand-up comedy that one. Ha ha. Anyway, I am getting better at English and it is not so bad in this place. And get this. We started out with only one English class a week and now there are two which is a bit weird but still OK by me.

We also do maths and science stuff and computers and agriculture even with chainsaws which is very upmarket. There's not many teachers coz there's not many boys here. Mr German does English and computers, and Mr Williams has maths and science, and Mr O'Neill is group-meister and school office, and Mr Sykes tries to teach us ag and outdoor stuff, and the Rev does sessions and office.

And there is Mr and Mrs Hartley who are the most fun. They are older than the other teachers and live at the school and they do the Shack, which is where we do live-ins but is better than a shack, but only a bit. Mr Hartley rules the bike shed and teaches us about fixing buckled wheels. He is always coming up with funny stuff to tell us like, 'It is a very bad idea to let a chainsaw know you are in a hurry.' I got my chainsaw licence pretty early so I must have been in a hurry but not showing it.

Mrs H teaches us food prep for live-in and camps. I reckon she worries about us a bit but tries not to show it. When Mrs H speaks softly we listen up.

The school is not too far out of town and looks like a big old farmhouse with some sheds close by. They are the shed for the camping stuff and the bike shed. It's all newer than it looks. The shack definitely looks old and is the shed from the original farmhouse which is where Mr and Mrs Hartley live.

The teachers all ride mountain bikes with us and when we are on camps we don't always know who is taking us each time. They do things differently around here.

In one of the campsites they have this ropes course where you climb up into tall trees and walk along the ropes to the next tree and it's about twenty metres up. Well, that's what it feels like. These ropes are so high that when we first tried it out Jacko said, 'I wish I'd listened to what my mum used to say when I was little,' and someone said, 'What did your mum used to say?' and Jacko said, 'I don't know, I never listened.' And that got us laughing coz everyone was nervous looking up at those ropes.

Anyway, on the high ropes we have a buddy who belays us, which means he holds a safety rope that runs through a gadget higher up in the trees so we won't fall if we slip off. When we do ropes we wear a harness that clips to the belay rope like we are full-on mountain climbers. It is fully technical. We are going to go rock climbing and abseiling once we get OK on the high ropes and that will be madaz.

These teachers are a bit above average somehow. I can answer a lot of the stuff already and I hardly ever go agro-biotic in class like I used to.

I like ag and we eat the stuff that we grow and there are some sheep and a calf that we look after. The sheep can be a pain coz they are dumb but the calf is more like having a dog, except for its shape and its size and everything else about it. Ha ha. The calf was a bull calf but it isn't any more since Mr Sykes got a bit bloodthirsty around his rear end.

He asked for help to hold the calf down when he did it and some of the other boys thought it was fun and helped him. Not me, though. And then Mr Sykes put his pocketknife back in his belt just like that. He uses that pocketknife when we are out on camp. I think my stomach is going to do something bad thinking about this. Time to change the subject.

We also keep chooks and they lay eggs that we eat. In the early days the chooks used to squawk and peck if they were still sitting on the eggs. These days we rule the chook-house. If we get to an egg when it's new enough we can carefully squeeze it into a different shape and that is cleverarity at its best I reckon.

I am still thinking about the calf. Hope it didn't hurt too much.

This kinesthetic thing is a bit much at times.

Clem.

SUNDAY, MAY 17
MERCY ME

Dear Gram

You know how I was talking about names and how Clement as a name was so seriously weird?

Well, I asked Dad why I got Clement. There must be no other person in the country called that. He got a bit upset and I was like, 'Here we go again, now I'm going to cop it.' But he didn't yell me out or anything. Told me I was named after my mum. Linda Clemency coz the oldest daughter always got Clemency as a second name. Said it's an old-fashioned word that means mercy. I got Clement because when

Mum died there would be no daughter. How come I didn't know all that?

Dad sure gets upset for a long time. But it's OK and he settled out of it and we played PlayStation like we haven't done for ages. I beat him good. Show no mercy. Ha ha.

So now I know. It's all good, like I've still got a bit of Mum after all. I hope so. Can't wait to hear Clem the Clam next, then I'll show no mercy.

I'm writing this early and today is going to be a great day. Mountain bike race this afternoon and I am going to be fully pumping it. Mr Rev with the fancy shockers, I might only have a hardtail but you are going to be copping it from Mr Merciful. Ha ha.

I wonder if I can get a mountain bike shirt with Show No Mercy written on it. That would be top gun.

Your merciful grandson,

Clem.

THURSDAY, MAY 21
LIFTING THE LID ON THE APRILIA

Dear Gram

I was in town again. It was busier than normal for some reason. People everywhere getting in the way. And you know what? I saw the Rev with a passenger on his Aprilia. It has got a seat after all. I thought the cover was for a toolbox or something. So how about that?

He was riding past with one of the kids on the back. The little boy looked like a koala hanging on real hard, kind of cute with this big helmet way bigger than his head could be coz he was only about ten. This time I waved and the little boy waved back as well as the Rev. That was good.

I wonder if I should call him Mr Paterson if I ever see him in town like that. This time he saw me and so I'm wondering what might happen in our session this time. How would it be if he said again, 'Tell me what you were thinking when you saw us ride past.' But I'm going to get in ahead of him. I'm going to say, 'Tell me what you were thinking when you saw me in the street on Saturday.' See what he says to that, eh? Ha ha.

The good thing is that I was just happy for that boy to have such a mega bike to ride around on and to have a dad like that. But I didn't choke up over it this time. I was sure glad that a bike like that has a seat for a passenger. Sure would be a waste of space if it didn't.

You know what? I can't figure out if I'd rather have a cool girlfriend or a hot motorbike. That Aprilia sure is a lovely looking lady. It's got to be a she, no bloke could look that pretty. And could you imagine a bloke with a name like April? That would be fully off.

Tell you what though, Augustus is a man's name and there is a motorbike called an Augusta Brutale. That bike is definitely a bloke. Couldn't have a girl named Brutal.

Hey, just thought of something. This beautiful girl named April marries a tough bloke named Augustus and they have lots of kids. They could call them names like Honda and Suzuki and Yamaha. Dumb joke there.

Anyway, I reckon it'll soon be time – again! – to put the hard word on Dad for a mountain bike with shockers front and back. Long travel, adjustable rebound, remote lockouts. Rock Shocks, that's what I want, girlfriend or no girlfriend. No passenger stuff for this dude, I'm fully into it when I'm pumping those pedals on that track. There's nothing like what happens to me out there when I'm racing and fully into it. See me on that road and don't expect a wave, I'm gone through the next corner as fast as I appear out of the last one. Way to go Gram.

Clem.

TUESDAY, MAY 26
OUT FOR THE COUNT

Dear Gram

The Rev did it to me again. Or I did it to myself more probably. We had our session and I said what I was going to say. I even practised it so I wouldn't get it wrong.

Started out with, 'I saw you on the motorbike.' And he said, 'I saw you too.' And I said, 'Tell me what you were thinking when you saw me in the street on Saturday.' Round one to Clem I reckoned.

But he said, 'That sentence sounds like you might have thought it up to say even before you got here today.'

I was like shocked and didn't know what to say right off and I said, 'Yeah.' It was like round two to the Rev.

So he said, 'You might even have practised it a bit so you wouldn't get it wrong.'

'Yeah,' again from me. How did he guess that? Round three down.

Then he said, 'What else could you have said today if you didn't say what you'd practised?' Round four and I was out for the count.

I really blew up and I said, 'That bike has got a passenger seat after all and that's just as well because if it can't take a passenger it's taking up too much space.'

And he said, 'Some people might think that a statement like that could refer to a person as much as to a motorbike. What do you reckon?'

And then I lost it fully toxic. Suddenly I was exploding angry and upset all at once and even without thinking if what he said was right or wrong I was like, 'That's just like how Dad is! Dad's like a motorbike that can't take a passenger,' and I was stalking around the room and hitting the wall and the door and everything and out of the window was the Aprilia sitting there in the car park. I could have gone out there and blasted it into the ground. And I was shouting out, 'My dad's got this cover over the passenger seat where I should be but he's still my dad and he should take that cover off.'

I was yelling and the Rev waited for me to get normal like he does whenever I chuck a hissy fit in the session. But this was the worst one ever. This was red-mist murderous.

Gram, it was horrible but that's how Dad is and how he's never had room. And I stalked around in the Rev's office and was going on about how I used to think up ways to hurt Dad even when I was little and I still do sometimes and I hate it when I get like that.

How did the Rev know all that? How did he know about that bike seat? Coz he was right, Gram. That's the worst part. I wasn't really talking about the motorbike at all. But when I saw the Rev on his bike with his little boy on the back I wasn't thinking all that toxic stuff, really I wasn't.

Gram, do you think there's a cover on me like there is on Dad? If there is the Rev sure got it off in that session. And I sat down again and cooled off and got back to normal, whatever that is. The Rev asked me what I wanted to do with the rest of the session and I didn't know. I was pretty washed up by all the toxic waste, and you know what we did? We went mountain biking.

'Let's get a couple of bikes from the shed and take one of the flat trails for a while.' That's what the Rev said. And so we got a couple of the school bikes and went for a ride in the bush. And when we got back I asked him if that was his son on the motorbike with him and he said next time he sees me in the street and he's on the motorbike like that he will stop and introduce me.

It's funny, Gram. He still didn't say who that boy was or anything. It's as if the Rev's always got this family kind of stuff covered up and I can't really see inside.

And that's where we left it. I think I need some time out from this stuff.

Clem.

FRIDAY, MAY 29
LITTLE PEOPLE

Dear Gram

Some things you have to hear straight off. A three day walk through the mountains. Mr Sykes proves, once again, that he is not the come-back king.

Walking this trail to the top of a cliff and there was a lookout up there with a fence and a long drop. Way across this valley was another lookout with a bunch of people, probably five or six people, a kilometre or more across the valley. Mr Sykes pointed to them and said, 'Wow, look at the size of those people over there.'

Jacko said nice and quiet, 'Probably the same size as us, I reckon.' Mr Sykes looked up and was about to say something but he couldn't think fast enough and stood there with his mouth a little bit open but his brain wouldn't take up the slack. And we stood around laughing like crazy.

And that's Jacko. He can be fully out there like when he does something that sends the teachers right off, or he can be almost silent and he just gets funnier. Still, I feel sorry for Mr Sykes on that one, he was goosed up proper.

That's it for me. Just another week of laughing and crying. Does this stuff ever end, Gram?

Clem.

MONDAY, JUNE 1
ONE HOT METAPHOR

Dear Gram

You know what I've been thinking? I've been thinking about what it might be like if I was writing to Dad instead of to you.

Trouble is, after that session with the Rev I kind of understand what he does to me when that cover goes onto his passenger seat. And if I was to be writing to him I think I would just try to yell my way through that cover and every letter would be the same. So I started to think what I can use to explain what he is like. And this is what they've been teaching us in school.

In English we learned that when something is like something else it can be a simile or a metaphor or an allegory or a symbol. A simile is when we say something is something else, and a metaphor is when we say something is like something else, and an allegory is when one thing is kind of hidden inside another thing.

So a simile is saying, 'The moon was a soft brush painting light across the bay.' How's that for romance? That's what happens when you have English after talking about girls all lunchtime. Ha ha.

And a metaphor is saying, 'The moon was like a beacon, drawing our love into its own embrace.' I got these lines from Hamish. Hamish thinks up romantic stuff easy, which means he's always talking about girls, which means I like to hang with him at lunch.

'As the moon rose across the bay my lady's love rose to illuminate the darkest places of my heart.' I'm on a Hamish roll here, Gram. Guess what I'm going to be like when I've got a girlfriend. Who cares about similes or metaphors anyway?

But that's not really what I was thinking about. Girls, I mean. Well I probably was a bit. OK more than a bit.

Though I was really thinking about writing letters to Dad. I want him to know what's happening in me. But my stuff is not love and moonlight, it's pain and darkness, and it keeps coming up from inside like lava. No way can I tell him this stuff. We'd be burned alive before I got it right.

Trouble is, I don't know if this is a simile or a metaphor.

Anyway, I wanted you to know that they are teaching us stuff in English, even though this school doesn't put too much energy into it like in a normal school.

Clem the Super-Heated.

Recipe For Disaster
Sorting out Brian the Brain

Live-in night before bushwalk.
Brian in the shower. Dusted chilli
powder inside his jocks.
Next day he got sweaty with
walking. Watching him squirm was
chillilicious. Yesss!!

'Hey Brian, looks like hot pants
suits you.'
'Hey Brian, they reckon you picked
up a hot date for tonight.'
'Hey Brian, you remember who sang
that song "Torture Me"?'
'Oh yeah, nearly forgot, Red Hot
Chili Peppers.'
Jacko knows something's up, but
this is personal.

WEDNESDAY, JUNE 3
JACKO DOES GERMAN

Dear Gram

I'm on a roll here. Must be starting to like English coz here's another story of what happened in English this week. Jacko's our class clown and a great bloke and I like him, even if he gets a bit high sometimes coz he's fully ADHD and on Rit and everything. At first meeting with Jacko you can tell there's a pretty wild party going on upstairs.

Well, we've been learning fancy words and stuff. How's this for a fancy word? Onomatopoeia. You ever heard of that? When Mr German started out on this Jacko said, 'Why use a big word when a diminutive one will do?'

Mr German's eyes give him away and we can tell when there's serious work happening inside. So, he looked at Jacko like something in there was saying, 'Is this going to be another one of Jacko's days?'

Now, the 'Onomato' thing means a word that sounds like its meaning. Tricky, that is, really tricky. So Mr German was trying to get us to think of words that sound like their meaning. He suggested some to start us off, like click and knock and smoooooth. So we started off to think of some, trouble was Jacko thinks faster than any of us and he stood up and said, 'I've got one.' And Mr German asked him what it was and he said, 'Faaarrt,' and at the same time he said the word niiice and slooow he let loose a beauty. We all laughed except Mr German coz that's how the world runs. And then the smell hit. He was radioactive. I reckon he must have specially prepared that one.

Mr German said, 'OK everyone outside while the air clears,' and he took us for a run around the sheep paddock and by the time we got back English was back to normal.

That was stand-up funny and that's how Jacko is and the teachers are mostly pretty patient about that sort of thing, but I guess it's not the worst thing that's happened in this school. We sure do a lot of laps around the paddock in this place.

One time Mr German asked Jacko to give him two personal pronouns and Jacko just said, 'Who, me?' Mr German thought for two seconds and said 'That'll do' and he went on to the next question for the next kid. Everybody looked at Jacko and said, 'What?' I think Mr German let him off the hook with that one. Probably just wanted to have an easy day.

Somebody should make a movie! He is the most fully serious mate I've got.

Clem.

THURSDAY, JUNE 4
MORE JACKO & OTHER STUFF

Dear Gram

Before you start thinking about Jacko like he's a hooligan or something, I should tell you that in this school kids like him are pretty normal. We've all had a tough time in normal school and some kids can't ever go back. I don't think Jacko is one of those kids, but some of the kids here are really off the planet.

There's kids with ADHD and on Rit or Dexies like Jacko and Pete. I don't have medication but Dad reckons I should be tested for ADHD, but I don't think I'm really doing it like those kids who seem to run full-boost turbo most of the day.

It's a bit like when I was in year six with this group of boys and we'd eat a stack of Redskins at recess and then be really off for the next hour or two. We'd be doing all this crazy stuff and saying crazy things. It was pretty nangtastic at the time and we had this competition to see who could be the first to make the teacher yell at him between recess and lunchtime.

Well ADHD kids are like that all the time, except they get it for free and we had to buy the Redskins.

Sometimes in group we talk about this stuff and we learned about this super-heated ADHD thing called Conduct Disorder which is CD and those kids mess up their lives coz they can't help it and sooner or later the coppers get them for something illegal. And if those kids can be kept safe from themselves then they can level out a bit and stay out of jail after all.

One time somebody's group camp finished up early because some kids set fire to Mr Sykes' tent. Seems Bundy & Co. wanted to get Mr Sykes back for confiscating a placcy bag of dope so they saved up the fuel for the Trangia burner. That night they poured it over his tent and lit it up. Mr Sykes must have come fizzing out of there fit to burn them in hell.

We were fired up in group about what to do to those guys, and Mr O'Neill asked us a question. 'What does real justice look like? Do we chuck a teenager in jail for something like this, or can we do something different?' It took us a bit of time but we mostly agreed that it's better for somebody not to have been in jail coz that can really count against you.

Drug stuff gets talked about around here, and the last time somebody got busted for dope he had to give a 'Don't Do Drugs' talk at lunchtime one race day when we had a visiting team. But that's another story and I've said enough.

These guys could have burnt Mr Sykes up bad and they still did it. I was so mad. Some of the boys here can be dangerous, but most are just kids trying to keep the lid on a volcano. Emotional problems are easy to find around here and I think that is where I am.

Another thing I have learned about is ODB which is Oppositional Defiant Behaviour which is when a boy just fights against everything. It doesn't matter if it's his dad or teacher or anybody, as soon as somebody asks him to do something he tells them to stick it. And ODB is what I feel like lots of the time and it is something that causes me grief.

But emotional problems come in all shapes and sizes and most kids are running on things that have happened to them when they were little. And ADHD and CD and ODB and EP are piled up pretty high at RV.

There's a couple of kids whose mum or dad or both have died or they've been adopted or something and they don't fit in anywhere. We've got one Koori kid who was adopted by a white family and they didn't know how to look after him properly and he kept running away. There's a Koori family who pick him up sometimes and I hope they are his relatives.

I think I'm a bit like him and I can see how not having a mum comes up in the way I think. And sometimes I almost say stuff about that teacher in primary school but that stuff is private and I just can't do it.

That thing with the teacher in year five is another thing that kids here have got, like I told you about Jacko and the Little Nipper coach.

That stuff really hurts and I don't tell anyone coz not even Dad believed me back then. Talking about that would be too much corrosion on me. I don't even talk about it around the campfire, but that's when I say a lot of other stuff.

Last time we were on camp I could even talk about Dad not having a passenger seat like I told the Rev. You know what, Gram? The other boys knew what I meant and everything. They can be really different around the campfire. It's like this place where people understand each other.

Mrs H says we choose between bridges or barricades. The campfire is where we build bridges.

Your hopeful grandson,

Clem.

SATURDAY, JUNE 6
ANOTHER METAPHOR BITES THE DUST

Dear Gram

It's race weekend. This time with visitors.

Sometimes we get to race a team from somewhere else, but it's hardly ever a team from another school. I don't know why they do it like that. Anyway, today we raced a team from the PCYC. Anything with the word police in it used to get me started, but the coppers have improved a lot since my time of trouble with them.

We've raced these PCYC kids before and I was bit nervous the first time, but the coppers don't come in uniform or anything. Some of their kids bring BMX bikes and even take them down the gully. That's pretty crazy I reckon but those kids can be deadly reckless I tell you. But I don't care how reckless they do it. I am going to wham into first place every time. Show me a good loser and I'll show you a loser, that's what I reckon.

Anyway, I'm always training for the team and I mostly get picked but not always coz they've got to get everybody in the mix if you know what I mean. I don't like it when I'm not in the team when I've done the work. And this week I got dropped, just like that. I was fully steamed when I found out, but they did this really weird thing.

Mr O'Neill got the guys who missed the team and took them for a special group session on another part of the track. We did some follow-the-leader where we had to stay in formation and as close to the bike in front as possible and things can get pretty hairy when you do it like that for too long. And after some follow-the-leader, Mr O'Neill ran a group.

Well, that group got pretty hot coz of the flak about not being picked in the races and Hamish said it was like waiting for his father to come and pick him up when it was his weekend but he never came. And I got really mad at his father doing that to him and you know what? Hamish got stuck into me for bagging out his dad. How weird is that? We're in group together and he never bags anybody out.

His dad's just like mine and he complains when I start saying it out in the open. Not only that, but he got so angry that he started crying and then everybody else just sat and stared at us. I was fighting off something inside myself but then it got a bit weird and it was like I knew what was going on inside him. We sat there and looked at each other and said nothing. There's too many kids in this place with all the same problems.

So Mike, that's Mr O'Neill, asked if there was something that somebody else wanted to say, but I was still running pretty hot. Some other kid said how his mum's boyfriend is like a father figure and I went off about that and was yelling back at him that what this world needs is not more father figures but more fathers.

'This world needs more proper dads,' I yelled. And that shut him up, but it got others talking and some of them were as hot as I was.

How does that happen? Do they have a factory for making dads where the mechanics in one section keep taking sickies and every dad comes out with the same bit missing? I reckon there's a bit that the factory puts in most dads that's like a magnet that sticks to another magnet in his son. But in this particular factory they forget to put the magnet in the dad and the son has nothing to stick to no matter how hard he tries.

I didn't think that up in the group. I really thought that up in maths class. Well, Mr Williams was going on yada yada yadaracious about stuff I'd never heard of. I can find my way anywhere out in the bush, but in maths I can hardly find the lowest common denominator. I reckon I come from a factory where they miss out the bit that makes numbers stay in order in the kid's brain, that's what I reckon. It's a simile. Or is it an allegory? I don't know what it is but it's the truth, I tell you.

We got back on the bikes and took turns in this thing like in the Olympics where the leader peels off each lap and goes to the back and the second boy becomes leader and the next lap it is the same until everyone has had a turn. We had to keep as close as we dared to the bike in front and the leader had to set a pace as fast as he reckoned the pack could keep to without getting dangerous. And that is the hardest time on the track that I have ever had.

Afterwards Mike asked us to say what position was the easiest and the hardest. I could see where he was going with this one (bit of visual speak there. Did you see it sneak past?), which was that it was probably the hardest to be in front and that's what a dad should be doing, being in front. But that was only in my head and I didn't say it out loud coz of Clem the Clam.

Trouble is, that idea was not coming from anybody else and I might have got it wrong. I spoke up about the front man being like the dad but nobody thought that was what we were really doing here. So I had to really think about what Mike had asked us and he started us off again with the question.

Most of the kids thought it was hardest to be the middle. The frontrunner gets to choose the path and there is nobody in the way. The backmarker doesn't have to think about anybody following him so he can be a bit slack. But in the middle you have to keep your eyes on the bike ahead and you have to remember that the bike behind might ram your wheel but you also have to be his leader.

And after all that Mike said, 'So, what do you reckon is the dad position?' Ha! I knew it. It's a metaphor, Gram. There's these dads and they are trying to follow how their dad and granddad did it. But they have to be leader to the son behind and the son might ram his dad's back wheel if he gets too impatient.

I reckon that is one heavy trip and Mike knew all along what was going to happen. Anyway, Mike is OK for keeping us on the track when we missed getting in the race team.

Couldn't believe it when he said it was time to get back coz the others would finish the BBQ. So we pumped those wheels like mad and we never cared who was leader or who was following and guess who was first back? You guessed it, not me, Hamish.

Hamish the romantic with the moon painting light and everything, but out on the tracks you should see him ride the flat stuff. I can beat him through the trees but he gets pumping like crazy on the fire trails and so he beat everyone back to where the races were just finishing up for the morning and they hadn't even started up the BBQ yet.

We stood around a bit and I said to Hamish, 'Sorry to stir you up out there.'

'That's OK,' he said. 'You were right about my dad anyway. Could have done without getting so upset, but.'

Suddenly we were talking about girls. He's got a one-track mind, that kid.

Your custom-made grandson, factory finished, limited warranty, ha ha.

Clem.

DVD Review in 100 words

'The Space Children'

The Shack screens another black and white classic from a forgotten era. A weird alien brain-blob helps a bunch of kids save the world from nuclear warhead rockets. The kids are the children of the space scientists who are making the rockets. One of the kids gets bashed up by his step-father and the alien blob stuns the step-father by thought power, so he goes and gets drunk and dies of shock. Some people just don't get it.

TUESDAY, JUNE 9

Dear Gram

Mostly I ride alone. My tyre tracks must be all over this place.

Was Mum that kind of person? Off by herself all the time? Even in the rain? Dad never says anything about her except to get mad at me. I reckon there's this pile of questions that should come standard and get answered when you are born, and this is one of them. I wonder sometimes if I am like her or not. How can I tell?

Maybe the questions will go around and around in my head and never slow up until I die. I hope not.

When I was out riding last weekend I decided to take some of the fire trails through the national park. Sometimes there are other people there and last weekend I got stopped by the park ranger. He was riding a mountain bike and it was a beauty. Carbon fibre handlebars, full shockers, schmick looking disc brakes, and more gears than I could see without getting down and counting them.

Anyway he waved me down and I was a bit scared coz that's never happened before. But he just asked, 'How are you going, mate?'

I said, 'OK.'

Then he asked, 'You from round here?'

How could I answer that? I didn't know if I should tell him I was from the school or not and I got stuck on that and he said, 'Are you OK?'

I said, 'Yeah I'm OK. I'm Clem and I'm from Rocky Valley.'

'You're pretty lucky to have that race track,' he said. 'I ride it sometimes and it's a great track.'

'You are lucky for having a job to ride a mountain bike around the national park.'

'I love this job. I get to check the fire trails and make sure people don't come in with cars or motorbikes.' And we talked about his bike which has twenty-seven gears and those disc brakes were hydraulics.

I was nervous but that bloke was OK in the end. He only wanted to talk mountain bikes. I get edgy when other people ask who I am.

So I need to know what Mum was like. If I am like her then I probably don't have to be like Dad. And you know what I don't want more than anything? I mostly don't want to be like Dad.

Thoughtful and lonely,

Clem.

WEDNESDAY, JUNE 10

Dear Gram

You know when I was little you were the only person I could talk with properly. I didn't know it back then, but I know it now. I suppose that's why, when the Rev reckoned I should write stuff, I started to write these letters to you.

What makes it so hard to talk to people anyway? I loved the way you listened back then. It was so good just to be a little kid with his gram. I would give anything to go back to being that all over again.

At this school people listen, most of them. I think I've even learned to listen a bit. What I mean is that sometimes I really get the feel of what another kid is saying, especially in group when we are all into the flow of it. Sometimes there is this buzz inside me and I'm glad to be there and I can talk easily and listen easily. And when that is happening I know that what I say is making sense and I understand what the others mean.

Sometimes though, Clem the Clam takes me over and I don't want to talk. You know what I've figured out about that? I've figured out that I talk the best when I know that the other person cares about me, that's what I've figured out, and nobody ever cared about me like you did. I remember one teacher way back somewhere who used to say that getting me to talk was like opening an oyster with a bus ticket. Well what I reckon is, you can open a clam with a bit of listening. My bit of talk for the day.

Clem.

FRIDAY, JUNE 12
THE FUNERAL, THE CLAM & THE BUS TICKET

Dear Gram

I've been thinking about the oyster and the bus ticket and that put me in mind of when they did the funeral for you and I didn't go.

I just knew that I would have to talk to people and they would talk to me, or Dad would say something, or he wouldn't say something, and I just didn't know what to do or how to handle it. So we were getting dressed for the church and I picked a fight with Dad and when he was angry enough I went yelling out of the house and grabbed my bike and rode away from there until I was lost in the traffic. Didn't even look back.

Dad must have been pretty worked up but I am only just starting to see it. I knew he would have to go to the funeral and not come after me. I sure left him carrying the can that day.

But what he didn't know is that I rode around and around until I got to your place. And then I went into the backyard and hid my bike between the bushes and the shed and I climbed up into my tree house and hid there. And the funeral was happening and I wasn't there.

I stayed in the tree house looking at the back

door and I knew the time would come when you would call out for me to come in for tea like you always did. But you didn't call. No matter how long I waited.

Dad came looking for me and was calling around the yard but I was not going to answer, no way, and then he kind of drooped onto the back step. He sat there looking up at the tree house for ages. I thought he must have seen me but I was in a war zone and I was not going to lose this one. When it finally got dark he left.

I knew that you wouldn't come calling out for me but still I waited for you to do it. Nobody could see me crying and somehow I went to sleep until the cold woke me up in the dark. I sat and shivered until the morning when you always opened up the back door. I knew it wasn't going to happen but I waited anyway.

When the time for opening the door was gone, I got down from the tree house and rode home and didn't say anything to Dad. I knew that I was as closed up as an oyster and all Dad had was a bus ticket. That is why you didn't see me at the funeral.

Three years later and I still hate myself.

Clem.

Mrs H Talks Food

Mrs H pinged me about Brian and
the chili daks. Must have been
something I said. Ha ha
Told her you can't make an
omelette without breaking some
eggs. She said, 'Here's something to
think about, Words get spoken like
eggs get broken.'
What is that, a test or something?

FRIDAY, JUNE 19

Dear Gram

It's Friday night and I'm sitting here at home.

It's not really home. It's just a house and sometimes I'm here and sometimes Dad is here and sometimes we are both here. Even if we're both here we don't share the same space. How do I even get close?

So I'm sitting here waiting for some mercy to come my way. And it's Friday night. How bad is that?

Anyway, I got this buzz of something inside me and I can't make it sit still long enough to understand it. All I know is that here I am in Dad's house and it's not really my place and not really my time. Well, my time better not be too far off. And that's it for Friday.

By now I must have a box full of bus tickets.

Clem the Thinking Clam.

SATURDAY, JUNE 20
INTER-GALACTIC SUPER-SATURDAY

Dear Gram

It's Saturday night and I am hungry. Man-o-man, am I hungry. I've already cooked up three of those chicken things with the butter and garlic inside and I am still hungry.

That's what love can do to you. Love, sweet love. Her name is Violet.

This morning I decided to wander around the shops coz Dad's place is pretty boring. Perhaps I'll see the Rev go past on his Aprilia with a little koala on the back. So I wandered around the plaza and I bought a smoothie. People everywhere in there and noise coming from all over, but all I could see was this one person sitting there in the smoothie bar. Violet. Long hair, soft and shiny. Eyes that I just wanted to look at. Saturday morning and there she was.

She was in my school last year, then I got kicked out. Well, Violet and me started talking about stuff and she was asking how I was going in my new school and I asked her how she was going in the old school and it was very laidback for a while there.

Then she started asking if there were any girls going to my school and I was like, 'No,' as if everyone already knew that but she didn't. So she asked me if I had a girlfriend and I said, 'No,' and then she asked me if I wanted to go with her. Just like that. Would I ever!?

And you know what? Clem the Clam appeared out of nowhere and I sat there wanting to say something but my brain went on holiday to Mars and I could feel myself getting red all over.

And you know what? She reached out and

grabbed my hand, not just grabbed it but held on to it, and she said, 'You can just nod if you like.' Then we started laughing and there was this buzz happening in me. I've never felt like anyone ever did that to me before.

My mouth was still running on daylight saving but then out came, 'You want to go to the movies?' And she said, 'Yes,' and that's what we did this afternoon.

Just as well holidays on Mars are pretty short but Violet is worth taking an interplanetary trip for.

I could tell you what we saw at the movies except I can't tell you. Ha ha. Yes I can, it was a little kids movie about a mouse. A new girlfriend and we go to a movie full of little kids and their mums. But there were teenagers all along the back row so we were pretty normal sitting there in the dark.

We held hands and I wondered if I should kiss her and I leaned in a bit and then I wondered if you should wet your lips a bit before you kiss a girl and if my nose was going to get in the way. I was glad all those little kids and their mums were facing the other way. I could feel Mars was coming closer, especially from the other kids sitting alongside me. What if they were watching? Anyway, I was warming up and hoped the movie didn't end before I got this right.

I don't know who worked out this kissing thing, but I reckon Violet was waiting for me and she kissed me back like there was no tomorrow. Except there is a tomorrow and we're meeting up again. Ha ha, and I am stoked.

So here I am thinking of Violet and I cooked up those chicken things from the freezer and I turned on the TV but I couldn't watch it and so I decided to have a shower and go to bed and think about tomorrow. And about Violet. But before that I am writing this. I sure hope this works out OK. I've got to be back at school on Monday.

Somebody is showing Clem some mercy. I love it here.

Clem.

TUESDAY, JUNE 29
MY LIFE AS AN ALIEN

Dear Gram

Well, here it is and it's Tuesday already. I thought I would get to write on Sunday night but I was floating all over the place and I just chilled out. I feel a bit intergalactic. The Force is with me. Ha ha.

On Sunday Violet and I met again at the smoothie bar. How about that, the onomatopoeic smoooothie bar. It makes me feel like I want to remember all that romantic stuff about the moon. Trouble is, I couldn't remember a single word of it, not even when Violet and I were in the movies on Saturday.

We didn't have money for too much and so we got a sub to share and then we just walked down to the park and around the little lake there about a zillion times. Violet is so awesome, she didn't want to do anything more than to just walk and talk.

Anyway, we met some other people from her school and we all just sat around. Clem the Clam was good to me this time and I got into the mix a bit. Doing groups at school has taught me something and it was like it never was last year. Even these people who I recognised from normal school just sat with us and we talked as if we were all normal. What I mean is, as if I was normal, and nobody said anything about me being chucked out.

So when we'd all gone back for a smoothie and Violet and I shared ours, I came back to Dad's place and she went home. Dad was home and he cooked tea and it was a bit different to tell him about Violet, and guess what he cooked. Chicken things with garlic butter in the middle. I thought that was so funny and I was laughing and he couldn't figure that one out. He must have a hundred of those things in the freezer.

So we watched TV for a bit but the inter-galactic thing was happening to me and I just fell into bed and must have gone off to Venus or somewhere coz suddenly it was Monday morning and I was on my way to school. This time Dad drove me which is pretty rare.

He's OK when he's onto it, Dad is.

Love from Clem in Love.

SECOND LETTER TONIGHT

Dear Gram

It's still Tuesday and I forgot to tell you about something really important. We had this English test. Mr German reckoned that we had to have a test sooner or later so let's just do it now. We were fully shocked but he was excellent about how he did it and we didn't have to write too much stuff coz some of the guys here don't write that well.

Mr German said we could set ourselves our own questions and then talk about what we reckoned and he would mark us OK as long as the questions we chose for ourselves weren't too easy.

Well, in this test I was going to do similes and metaphors, coz I wanted to say something about the weekend and Violet and how she is fully Ultra and the moon painting romance across the bay.

All that romantic stuff about the moon got me going and I was talking about similes and metaphors to the class and you know what? I got it wrong. I had them all the wrong way round. Probably from the beginning. But the worst bit is I sure did make a mess of trying to tell everyone about Violet.

The other guys think it's fully stand-up comedy when I goose myself but I wouldn't want to do that, not with Violet liking me like she does.

Do you think that's OK, Gram? This romance stuff sure isn't like I thought. How do they do it so easy on TV? Another stupid question from Clem the Clown.

So that was how I got to tell everyone about Violet but it wasn't all bad coz some of the kids have asked me about her and I've been more careful and I just say she is fully nice and we've been to the movies and shared a smoothie and that she likes me.

Pete has a girlfriend but he keeps kind of quiet, so that is what I'm going to be like about Violet. Pete is laidback about his girlfriend and at lunch he asked me about Violet, but not too much or anything. I told him about how she held my hand and said, 'You can just nod if you want to,' when I couldn't think of anything to say. And he laughed coz it was funny but he didn't bag me out.

He asked me what her name was and I said Violet and he said, 'I know that, dummy, you told us in class. What's her other name?'

I had this big grin and said, 'Her other name is Ultra.'

Pete said, 'Violet Ultra? You got to be kidding, man.'

'Her full name is The Ultra Violet.'

Pete laughed and punched my shoulder and said, 'You are the full fruit loop, dude, what's her surname?'

'Carter, Violet Carter.'

'Violet Carter?' he said. 'She wants to go with you? That is the best thing, man. My girlfriend goes to school with her and she is very OK.'

So I asked what his girlfriend's name was and he said Caitlyn and I said that it was a pretty name, but then up from inside came Linda Clemency and it got me running hot a bit inside.

And Pete said, 'Are you OK? You look a bit funny.' And I said I was OK but I had just thought of something. And that made me very careful so I punched him on his shoulder and we fooled around like that for a bit and it stopped the talk of girls' names straight off.

I reckon that I want to talk about Violet like she will be some kid's mother one day, you know what I mean? I wouldn't want someone from the past to suddenly appear and to talk about how once my mum was his girlfriend and to say things about her that I wouldn't want to hear. That's what I reckon about Violet.

It's just as well this is a live-in night for me coz here it is after midnight and I'm getting sad when I wanted to tell you about Violet and she's not sad at all. Lucky for me I don't have to make it to the bus tomorrow coz I never would being up this late writing. And this is my second letter in one night. That's pretty amazing.

I think I'll go back to where the moon is painting romance across the bay. I've got to get that stuff right for when I say it to Violet. Ha ha.

From Clem the Romantic.

Mr Hartley Gets Serious

Mr Hartley says you can fool some of the people all of the time. Or you can fool all of the people some of the time. But you can never fool Mrs H.

Well shizzle my nizzle.

FRIDAY, JUNE 26
HOW DO YOU HOLD A GIRLFRIEND?

Dear Gram

I've been thinking about Violet, and this is what I want to know. How do you hold a girlfriend? Like, how do I keep her as my girlfriend without making a mess of things, coz that's so easy for me to do. Especially when it comes to people.

This morning I was getting breakfast and there was this big tub of yoghurt in the fridge. Wild Berry, my favourite. Anyway it had this see-through clip-on lid and I was getting breakfast ready and I got the yoghurt from the fridge and just as I closed the door the yoghurt dropped like mad coz the lid had come off the tub and I was holding it by the lid.

That yoghurt took about a millionth of a second to get to terminal velocity and it hit the floor fast and suddenly there was this wild berry fountain all up the fridge and everywhere.

OK, so you can't blame gravity when you fall in love. But something's got to be to blame for some of this.

So, how do you hold a girlfriend? Was it this hard for you way back when, Gram?

Love from Clem.

SATURDAY, JUNE 27
VIOLET IS A LEGEND!

Dear Gram

Violet is so a legend. We met up for another smoothie. This could be habit forming. Ha ha. And then this amazing thing happened. We were just coming out of the plaza when this red motorbike pulled up in the street. Guess who? Yep, the Rev with a passenger, the little koala. Ha ha.

He waved to us after he stopped the bike coz he had to steer it backwards into the gutter to park it and everything. And then he tapped the little boy on the knee a couple of times, which must be the signal to hop off coz that is what the kid did and they took their helmets off and the Rev said, 'G'day Clem' to me. And the little boy turned out to be a little girl, about eight or nine and wearing boots and Levis and a little leather jacket and everything.

And there we were, Violet and me together and I was like, what do I do now?

And the Rev was very laidback and he said, 'Hello Clem, this is my daughter Emily. Emily, this is Clem who is a friend of mine.'

So I said, 'G'day, Emily,' to Emily and then I just stood there wondering what to do next and the Rev said, 'Aren't you going to introduce us?' And suddenly I remembered Violet and I said, 'This . . .' and that was as far as I could go because my voice did this squeaky thing like it hasn't done to me since year seven and I sounded like somebody in the mouse movie. It took a couple of goes for me and I finally said, 'This is Violet,' and, 'This is Mr Paterson, but we all call him the Rev.'

Violet said, 'Hi Mr Paterson, hi Emily.' She was so the best about it and I was full-on proud, squeak included, but I could have done without the squeak in that situation and that's the truth.

And then Emily said, 'Daddy and me are going to the Mouse Movie,' and she looked up at the Rev and then said, 'Daddy and I are.'

Emily had this big grin and Violet said, 'We saw that last week,' and the Rev looked at me and he grinned and he said, 'Was it fun for you?' And you know what I did then? I went off to Mars again and got all red and couldn't say anything coz I was remembering Violet and me in the movie and kissing and everything.

Violet said it was a great movie and she hoped Emily had a nice time and off they went with their helmets swinging in their hands and I had to shut my eyes for a bit and Violet was genius with that and she suddenly put her arms around me and hugged me full-on and then she kissed me right there in the street. Incredimacious I can tell you.

I looked at the Rev's Aprilia and it had the pillion seat on now and you know what Gram? The seat is always there and the cover just clips over it and it looks a bit like a racing bike when the cover is on there, almost as if it can make a faster getaway when the passenger seat is covered up.

Violet thought the bike was pretty smart but not really her thing she said coz she's a girl and I said that Emily was a girl and she looked fully cute with the helmet and the jacket. So Violet said, 'Yeah she did, didn't she?'

I asked her if she knew what her name meant and she said it means Violet like the colour and the flower and I said I reckoned her name was pretty Ultra and so was she. She laughed at that coz it was a compliment and I was being nice as well as a bit funny. And I told her that my name means mercy and she didn't like, laugh at it meaning mercy, but she laughed and said, 'No kidding?'

I told her that I was thinking of getting a mountain bike shirt that says, 'Show No Mercy!' and we both laughed. Violet knows that I want to be OK instead of merciless.

Except on the bike track, that is. When I am out there and I am in the zone I am out to win over everybody, no matter what. And also Dad except when he's going off at me. And to some of the teachers at my old school, well most of them actually. And especially one of them.

And then it was time I started thinking of something different and so I just left it. Just like that I stopped thinking about it. I didn't know I could do that. I think that was because Violet makes me think differently.

And then something really strange happened. I got this buzz inside and said, 'Let's go and do something that I'm thinking of.' And she said, 'What is it?' And I said, 'A surprise.' And we went back into the plaza to this store that sells chains with beads and little feathers and I spent my movie money on a bracelet with little glass beads in all different purpley colours. She said it was really sweet and when she said 'sweet' I got this buzz inside all over again as well as going off to Mars and getting red but I could still talk this time and I said I was glad she liked it and I called it the Ultra Violet Bracelet coz of the purple.

Gram, that is the smartest thing I said all day and it was the best Saturday. I can't remember much because I keep thinking of the bracelet and how Violet said she liked it.

Got home and Dad was already there and so we cooked some tea together. Mostly he makes such a mess. I guess having to do that stuff at school camps has taught me something. Another triumph for Mrs H.

So that was my Saturday, Gram. I told Violet I would call her when my week slowed up coz I had bike racing on Sunday and then live-in for the two-day group camp.

We did the washing up together this time instead of me doing it all. Dad's OK sometimes.

Ultra Clem signing out.

SUNDAY, JUNE 28
THE BIKE IS NOT MY FRIEND

Dear Gram

The race day was not good. I spilled coming down the gully and lost the final. Well, came in third and I was in front until then. The worst thing is that this really dangerous kid named Nick won the final. Nick is like Kryptonite and radioactive and if he is around I know things are not going to turn out good.

I even put on speed down the gully because of him, but there's this tree root asleep across the track. Nick was behind me but still on my mind and the bike didn't hop over the tree root like it normally does. So I went skittering down among the rocks.

'You're not my friend,' I said to the bike.

Well that didn't get me very far. And there was no help coming from the tree root. Or the gully. It's just me against everything. Me against the track. Me against Nick and all the others. Even me against my own bike. When you're on your own, you're on your own.

Who put this stupid world together anyway? I could have won that race easy.

Clem.

Recipe For Disaster

Sorting out Brian the Brain

Remove paper label from ring-pull can of dog food, cut can around middle, clean out the dog food. Chop up Maltesers, Kit Kat, a Mars bar or two, nuke for a few seconds, mix it sloppy with some caramel topping and refill the can. Tape it up strong and replace label. Took it to camp, popped the top, grabbed a fork and started eating. Brian took the dare but I had a spare can in original condition. Who needs Jamie Oliver's school dinners?

WEDNESDAY, JULY 1
RAP-RUNNING

Dear Gram

Two-day group camp is over. Just the five of us with Mr Sykes. What a blast. It's called the Ridgy Didge camp coz we went abseiling off the Ridgy Didge which is the biggest cliff around here. Group camp means no ferals like Bundy or Nick who can set me off, and not only me but everybody. Brian can be a feral sometimes, but at least he's our own feral, ha ha. And I sure got him with that dog food tin. That was fun-city that was. Brian's not all bad, but. It's just that he works so hard at showing his worst side. Trouble is, his worst side is bigger than any other side of him, ha ha. I'm on a roll here.

Anyway, back to the camp. It's Hamish and Pete and Jacko and me and Brian. We started the walk-in even before the sun was up and still Mrs H had us up getting a proper breakfast. Mrs H is like nobody else I tell you, doesn't she ever sleep? We got up to the Ridgy Didge about lunchtime and set up camp. Then we abseiled for the rest of the afternoon.

The Ridgy Didge is all tree roots and saplings at the top and is running wet from a continual soak. You can see nearly forever from the rocks up behind the cliff top, but we are there for the long look down, and for the ropes. It's the hottest abseil site we've been to and everybody was a bit nervous that first afternoon. It sure had us steamed up looking down through those saplings. It takes a full seventy-five metre rope to get down, so we started out careful and took things slow and steady.

Between the saplings and the wet rock-face and the boggy mud at the bottom it sure made us concentrate. I suppose that's why we finished that first day so worn out. And being worn out can make some people vulnerable, like what happened to Hamish.

We got a fire going and put the billy on and started to change our wet socks. Everyone was talking about the buzz of the abseiling and Hamish made this funny grunting noise that stopped us straight up. We looked around and he's gone all white and staring into the ground. Actually, staring at his foot. His sock is bright red. A whole lot of it. And the blood is starting to flow up over his boot which he's got half undone.

We all sat there staring and Mr Sykes said, 'Let's look at what you've got there.' Hamish was starting to sag a bit. Mr Sykes slowly pulled off the boot. The sock was red with blood from top to toe. Mr Sykes tipped that boot up and more blood just ran from it. There must have been half a coke can of blood in there. Hamish started to fall forward and we had to hold him up. 'Get him a cup of tea, somebody,' said Mr Sykes. 'Hamish, put your head down between your knees. You'll be OK in a minute.'

Pete got him some tea and Hamish sat up again. Mr Sykes said, 'OK, my little beauty, where are you?' and he slowly peeled Hamish's sock off his foot. Sitting inside that sock was the biggest leech I have ever seen. It was fat as the abseil rope and must have been sucking Hamish's blood for half the afternoon.

'You must have picked him up in the boggy stuff at the bottom of the cliff,' said Mr Sykes. 'He's had a good feed and you've been bleeding into that sock for a long while. Clean your foot up and we'll see where he got stuck into you.' So Hamish got cleaned up and patched and Mr Sykes chucked the leech into the bushes and the rest of us were very careful about pulling our boots off I can tell you.

Hamish was still pretty white, but at least all that blood had an answer that didn't require stitches. We stirred Hamish up a bit about nearly fainting, but he wasn't up to it and just gave us the evil eye.

Then Mr Sykes said, 'You know the difference between a leech and a lawyer?' Quick as anything Jacko says, 'A leech stops sucking you dry after you're dead.' We all look at him and he says, 'My dad's favourite joke after the divorce.' Mostly he has this quiet smile when he does this, but this time it was a different story. So now we had two people under their own little cloud and that hot abseiling talk was fading fast.

We cooked up our tea and then it was time to get the campfire going. I had the dog food tin in my backpack, waiting for the right moment. Just enough light, just enough dark, just enough Brian. I couldn't believe it when he took the dare, but it was another story when he realised what I was eating. So then we had three people under their own little cloud, and I was wondering what was really happening out there. Sleep didn't come easy after all that.

The next day we were to abseil for the morning and walk back after lunch. We got to the cliff and things were different. I reckon it was partly the dog food, and partly the leech, and partly the lawyer joke.

We did normal abseiling the day before, but this time Mr Sykes said he was going to get us rap-running. Rap-running means face-forward down that cliff and we've done it on smaller drops. The Ridgy Didge has got lots of reasons for not rap-running, like those saplings and the water running down the rock.

We got set up and first to go was Hamish. He was off down that cliff like nobody's business and we just watched him go for it. Jacko was belaying and he was cheering him down the cliff like crazy and trying to keep up with the belay rope. Hamish unclipped at the bottom and then Pete charged off. Nowhere near as reckless. Brian clipped on and he was out to break something, either a record or his neck. He made it quick to the bottom and Hamish and Pete were cheering him on. I set off and was madaz nervous but this was a test of dog food and I was not about to lose. And all the way they cheered me down, even Brian. Jacko had started out belaying and he went to the top and clipped on. Watching him come racing through those saplings was amazing and suddenly he was standing beside us amongst the noise.

Mr Sykes was checking our set-up at the top and we were taking turns belaying from the bottom. That rap-running was the adrenalin rush of the decade and we kept up the speed for most of the morning. We were like the SAS on secret training out there in the bush. The worst part was running back to the top coz that track up around the cliff was getting longer each time. We spent two hours rap-running that cliff and by the time we finished up we'd cheered equal to a footy final.

We packed up at lunchtime and the walk down out of the mountains was a bit quicker coz we were still so hyped up. So it proves that all you need is one boot full of blood, an old lawyer joke, and a can of dog food and you can do anything you set your mind to do. They never taught me that in my old school.

Loving it here,

Clem.

FRIDAY, JULY 3
SUDDEN DEATH

Dear Gram

I can't believe it. The Rev's bike has gone. The Aprilia. The 1000R. Gone. Up in smoke. We watched it. All of us. We just stood there and watched it burn away.

My mind keeps going back to the camp and the rap-running and there's a teacher up the front going on about something and suddenly there's all this happening.

We were in maths or English or something. Just before lunchtime. There was a noise and somebody yelling and it got pretty frantic real quick. We rushed out and could smell the fire and there in the car park was the 1000R. Burning like mad with smoke rising black and twisted.

The Rev already had the fire extinguisher and he was hot to trot with that thing, but it did no good. That bike was fibreglass and plastic and petrol and it was too late to save it. We all stood watching and then it really went up.

That petrol tank must've got so it couldn't take any more coz there was a loud rush and serious flames started shooting everywhere. The bike turned itself into something very angry and everyone ran for cover.

The hissing and roaring of it was awesome. It was like it was never going to stop and we could feel the heat through our clothes from the edge of the car park. The office wall is all blistered paint, and my face will be scorched for days, I reckon.

Some of the kids were saying things like, 'Burn, baby, burn,' and, 'You could do some hot laps now, Rev.' But they got shut up by the rest of us. Even Bundy. I've never seen Bundy get shut up before. But this time he took it. Outnumbered.

When the fire truck arrived there was not much for them to do except hose down the wreckage. The whole school smells of smoke and the car park looks like a war zone.

That Aprilia has got me thinking some serious stuff this year and I don't know what I'll do without it sitting out there in the car park.

Clem.

SATURDAY, JULY 4
TWO-UPPED

Dear Gram

I was out riding and this strange thing happened. There was this noise and when I looked around there were two people following me. I didn't recognise them but they were bigger than me and were trailing me by fifty metres.

I was fully nervous when I realised what was going on. Sometimes on weekends there are other riders in the national park, but this was just in the bush away from the race track and there are hardly ever other people in that part. I started to speed up to get away from them but they kept the same distance on my tail and I was starting to worry about whether they were trying to give me a bit of a scare or something.

Some people are like that and we get kids who come into the tracks to find someone from the school and pick a fight for no reason. That sucks but it is how some knuckle-draggers do it.

Then I thought that I could ride to where the track gets worse or even ride down the gully and shake them off. Trouble is I didn't know if they could ride me out or not.

Then I did a really strange thing. I just stopped and let them catch up to me. I guess I figured that if they were going to do something then I probably couldn't get away anyway. So I just stood there as they kept coming closer. And they both watched me and they slowed down a bit but they kept on riding past.

So I don't know if I spooked them or what was going on. Anyway, I watched them ride on a bit and one of them turned around to look behind and I got on the bike and raced through the bush until I got closer to school.

I still haven't got around to speaking with Dad about a new bike. Hydraulic disc brakes would be good, and lock-out shocks. And what about XTR shifters? I can't figure out what's hardest, asking Dad about another bike, or watching the Rev's Aprilia burn, or those guys shadowing me today.

Your loving grandson,

Clem the Undecided.

SUNDAY, JULY 5
FOLLOWING ME IN HIS MIND

Dear Gram

Those guys following me yesterday still have me spooked. And you know what I think about whenever I see those two in my memory? I think about that teacher in primary school again.

I reckon that man used to follow me in his

mind and I could feel it. He used to say, 'Show me your muscles,' and then he flunked me and I had to repeat that year. I didn't even have muscles, and he followed me in his mind and did things to me that I can't tell you about and that even Dad wouldn't believe. Two years running he followed me in his mind.

And those two guys keep putting that teacher and his two years into my head.

Clem.

TUESDAY, JULY 7
SURVIVING BUNDY

Dear Gram

I'm a bit on the mend, but my head still hurts. I reckon I've got a broken head but the doctor calls it concussion. Whatever it is, I don't like it. And my eyes don't like it especially. And it's all coz of that burning of the 1000R.

The coppers reckon somebody burnt it deliberately. After the fireys came the cops turned up, and guess what they found? A Trangia burner. Inside the bike somewhere. Tucked away. Somebody set that burner going. An hour later, bomb dot com.

The story about that burner has gone viral. There was a bunch of us out at the paddock talking about it. Bundy stuck his finger into his other fist and said, 'When you know where to put your thing, mate, that baby's banjaxed. Nobody's going to want to ride her any more.' Everybody laughed but I looked at him for a bit and suddenly I got it. So I went for him.

I must have got in a couple of good punches, but when I woke up it was all over. My head got the worst of it. Don't know how long it took. Mr Sykes was looking at me there on the ground.

'He fell off the fence, Mr Sykes,' somebody said.

'There was a bunch of us sitting there and he started laughing at something and went over backwards, Mr Sykes.'

'Clem the Clumsy, that's what happened, Mr Sykes.'

I tried to sit up and I was going to have it out with whoever said that stupid thing but sitting up didn't work and Mr Sykes took their story. They got me inside and somebody thought it would be a good idea to take me to the hospital to check me out.

From Clem.

Questions They Ask When We Stuff Up

What happened?

What were you thinking of at the time?

What have you thought about since?

Who has been affected by what you have done? In what way?

What do you think you need to do to make things right?

WEDNESDAY, JULY 8
ONE BANANA SMOOTHIE AND
FOUR STRAWS

Dear Gram

I just spoke with Violet on Dad's phone. I didn't say anything about the thing with Bundy. Some things are different these days. Even over the phone I can feel her beside me, her long hair on the breeze, eyes dark and deep. She is so incredible.

Dad's real pleased about Violet and you bet that makes me glad. He hasn't mentioned Lyndal for ages but I'm OK about that. She works in the same place as him and perhaps they weren't all that serious and I got it wrong.

I am in the zone with Violet. Her mum and dad want us all to go to lunch sometime. Maybe I'll take them to the smoothie bar and we can all share the smoothie this time.

'One banana smoothie and four straws please.' Ha, ha.

I'm signing off.

Clem.

THURSDAY, JULY 9
THE SESSION OF SECRETS

Dear Gram

Session with the Rev.

'Clem, I've got something important to discuss. Do you mind if I come straight out with it?'

'OK,' I said. He was very straight up this time.

'Of all the people you could have picked a fight with, why Bundy?'

Out of nowhere I said, 'Sometimes you have to dance on the battlefield.'

He looked at me with that raised eyebrow thing and I said, 'I don't get it either, but it's the truth. And anyway, that bike owed me something and if anyone was going to burn it down it should have been me.'

The Rev just looked at me and said, 'Uh huh.'

Then I looked at him and said, 'How did you know about Bundy and the fight?'

And he looked at me and said, 'How did you know about Bundy and the fire?'

And I said, 'I reckon the coppers have got a bit of fingerprinting to do among the Trangias and I've seen Bundy's hands close up and I reckon I've probably got those same fingerprints on my skull.'

The Rev had this secret smile that he

sometimes gets like when something is going down in class but he already knows about it.

Then I said, 'What do I do if Violet finds out?'

And he said, 'I'd also be a bit worried about Mrs H if I were you.'

Short. Sharp. Session over.

Anyway, my eyes are looking in the same direction as each other so the concussion must have eased up.

Holidays next week so I'd better be looking straight. Extra time with Violet and I don't want to miss a single blink.

Love from visionary Clem.

SATURDAY, JULY 25
THE CLAM OPENS UP

Dear Gram

Violet and me have spent a lot of time together on these holidays. This week we went out with her mum and dad. They are really nice. But I was still a bit nervous about the Bundy fight and what if I say something stupid. Needn't have worried.

We met at the smoothie bar and I ordered 'one banana smoothie and four straws'. Even the guy behind the smoothie bar broke up and I didn't even get to Mars on that one but I was on fire on the inside like the old redskin days.

So we had our smoothies and I ordered Wild Berry coz I remembered the yoghurt and my question about how to hold on to a girlfriend. Violet had my favourite, banana, which was really excepto of her, so I sneaked in another straw and we laughed about that. And her dad even paid for them all.

They don't know my dad but they know the place where he works coz the head office is right there in the main street and I said that he goes away for work a lot, but not much since Gram died. Then what I just said caught up to my ears and I had to stop talking and so they stopped talking too.

And now I can start writing again coz I had to stop writing for a bit there. I was up front about school because it is such a madaz place and I said that normal school found me hard to handle but this one is OK. And I told them about the bike track and the races and Violet's dad said that it all sounded very positive.

Violet's mum really likes that I bought her the bracelet. And Violet was wearing it, which made me smile inside as well as outside.

Then something mad happened. We finished the smoothies and Violet's dad said, 'How about we go out for a nice lunch?' And I was OK about that and thought we'd get a sub, but we went to this place where they put menus on the table for you. Mr Carter said, 'Let's just order a bunch of stuff and share it around.' and that's what we did. So we had prawns and fish pieces and spring rolls and little bowls of sauce to dip it all in and they had the coldest Coke I have ever had. And even though it was only lunch we didn't leave there for ages and we were talking through it all.

And they asked me more about school and so I went in headfirst. And I told them that we learned about lots of things apart from bike racing like metaphors and onomatopoeia and rap-running and things that normal school never taught me.

When I was talking Violet's mum and dad were smiling and sometimes they would give each other a quick look with a grin. I didn't like the quick looks so much but I liked it when they smiled. My dad could take a lesson from them.

It was like 'Clem the Clam Opens at The Opera House' which is a visual joke, Gram, can you see it? I've never spoken so much even in group, but Violet was there and when she smiles I just open up. Still, I hope her mum and dad didn't think I was off or anything.

That bracelet must be the smartest thing I've ever done.

Love from Redskin Ready Clem.

WEDNESDAY, JULY 29
SOME THINGS YOU HAVE TO FIND OUT FOR YOURSELF

Dear Gram

Time to get high. We did the high ropes course again. It's the best fun but when we started out I was nervous as. We have to climb up rope ladders to get to the walk rope, and have you ever tried to climb a rope ladder? It's madaz coz they keep twisting and running away from your feet.

We've been asking for ages how high the ropes are but Mr Sykes won't tell us.

'One day we'll have to get to that,' is what he keeps saying. So this time we were asking him again and somebody said, 'Why don't we measure it?'

Mr Sykes said, 'That's a good idea, how are you going to do it?'

Nobody could think of anything straight up until Pete said, 'Why not get a bit of string and let it down from the ropes to the ground and then we can run the string along the ground and step it out?'

Mr Sykes smiled at Pete and said, 'You know? You could give that a go.'

But Jacko, being Jacko, looked straight at Mr Sykes and said, 'That won't work.'

Mr Sykes said, 'Why not?'

Whacko Jacko said, 'Because we want to know how high it is, not how long it is.'

We all started straight up laughing coz Jacko had done it to Mr Sykes again. Mr Sykes had been holding off telling us how high the ropes were until we came up with how to measure it for ourselves. They do that a lot around here, but I reckon Jacko and Pete cooked up this little plan to set him up.

Mr Sykes started laughing with us and then he said to Jacko, 'For that you can be the one to climb up the ladder with the string.' And he took this roll of string out of his pocket which had been there all along. And now I don't know who was setting up who.

This place is pretty nangtastic. And you know what? That roll of string was just long enough to reach the ground and Mr Sykes must have had it in his pocket every time we were on the high ropes, just in case somebody came up with Pete's suggestion.

Mr Sykes sure got the laugh on that one, but Jacko is still the funniest kid in the place and Mr Sykes said that nobody had ever come up with that joke since they built the ropes course, which is a neat thirteen metres from the ground.

Then I said, 'They chose that for the height

coz that's the only piece of string Mr Sykes had in his pocket at the time,' and that was fully stand-up for everyone and Mr Sykes laughed like he was one of us.

Then Jacko put on Mr Sykes' voice, which he does so easy and said, 'You boys know that asking questions is not the only way to find the truth.'

Jacko grinned at me and I knew we were on and I said to him, 'Mr Sykes, if a boat is made of steel how does it float?'

And Jacko did Mr Sykes again, 'I dunno.'

So I said, 'Mr Sykes, how do fish breathe underwater?'

'I dunno.'

'Mr Sykes, if air is invisible why is the sky blue?'

'I dunno.'

'Mr Sykes, do you mind me asking all these questions?'

'Course not. You don't ask questions, you don't learn nothin'.'

Well that was it for everyone but Mr Sykes tried to bust into everyone's laughing and said, 'OK you guys, let's get some work done here, we've had enough jokes for today,' and that is when Jacko put on this little English kid's voice and said, 'Please sir, don't you want some more?' which is from a DVD of Oliver Twist we did at the Shack and there is a Mr Bill Sykes Twist in there.

And that fully finished high ropes coz we all got fully moxied laughing and even Brian the Brain and I had to lean on each other to stay up and there was too much stupidivity for anything off the ground that day.

Mr Sykes could see that we would be flat out dangerous on the high ropes with all those jokes coming from us, and so he took us back to the paddock and we did blind running, only this time it was backwards and that is how Mr Sykes got his own class back from Jacko and Pete and me.

I will tell you about blind running in a second but first I have to say something about measuring those ropes. No other group has ever said anything about knowing how high they are. Now I'm starting to wonder if we got to it first or last coz none of us are going to tell the other groups. They have to do that for themselves. That's how it is.

But what if Mr Sykes won't have to carry that string any more coz we were the last? That would be fully obnoxified, being the last to get it I mean. And you know something? We will have to live with never knowing if we got to it first or last.

There are probably heaps of things that we

will only find if we go looking. I might leave here with lots of things that I haven't learnt just because I didn't think to go looking. My head hurts when I think like this.

We started out walking the ropes pretty carefully and everyone was nervous but after a few times we were all getting fully fierce with how we ran the course at high speed and even backwards sometimes. Backwards is full-on mad coz you have to watch your feet and down there is the ground, and thirteen metres might be one thing when you lay a piece of string along the ground but when you are looking down from those ropes it is a very different piece of string I can tell you.

Back to blind running, which is a trust-yourself thing like the ropes but it is in the paddock. We take the sheep out first coz they are so dumb and would get in the way. Everybody stands evenly around the paddock fence. Each boy in turn has to clamp his eyes shut and run as fast as he can, which can be very toxic on some people, and he runs until he reckons he has to open his eyes or die.

Most boys can get about halfway across the paddock before they have to stop. If they start to run too close to the fence then the other boys around the edge yell, 'Stop.' But there is no shame in not running straight and I reckon some guys have one leg longer than the other coz they keep turning off in the same direction every time.

Mr O'Neill says the ropes and the blind running teach us lots of things like depth perception and spatial imagination and several different kinds of trust and propriocentricity and other casual stuff like that. Ha ha. And you know what? I'm not even going to tell you what that fancy P word means. Some things you just have to find out for yourself.

Love from Cryptic Clem.

Not Quite a DVD Review

The latest excitement from The Shack, home of black and white. Mr and Mrs Hartley showed us a DVD of what remains of the world's first feature movie. It's the story of Ned Kelly and was made about 100 years ago. Soon after it came out the coppers banned all bushranger movies in Victoria and NSW.

This is what is meant by the silent movie era

MONDAY, AUGUST 3
THE HAMISH MESSAGE

Dear Gram

We had English and Mr German gave us a few sentences and we had to write something with that as the beginning. The sentence Jacko and I had was, 'He felt great anguish in his heart'. That was it. Not much to go on is it?

Anyway, Jacko started up with Mr German and he was working up to something funny, but he never got to finish it coz the Rev came and called Mr German out of the room. They came back in again and it was pretty clear that something serious was going down.

The Rev came to the front and said, 'Boys, we got some bad news this morning. Very bad news for us all.' Everybody went kind of quiet. 'The bad news is that Hamish died last night.' We all just sat there looking at the Rev. Nothing happened.

I checked around the room. He wasn't there. Everybody checked. He still wasn't there. We kept glancing at each other.

Somebody said, 'Bundy's not here either,' and that started off the yelling.

'That can't be true. Not Hamish.'

'No way, man. That's wrong.'

'You better go check your bleedin' facts, Rev,

coz this is a bad place for a joke.'

'Frak, man, that is so off.'

We got louder and louder and the yelling was coming from everybody until we filled that classroom with f-bombs.

Nick stood up quick and his desk went flying and he went for Mr German.

'You blit-brain,' he yelled. 'You put them sentences up there on purpose and now look what's happened to Hamish. Call yourself a teacher? You dunno dog-shit.' Everybody shut up. I guess Kryptonite becomes a way of life.

It was the Rev who spoke. 'Nick, what you said shows that you care about Hamish. We see that. We all feel it.' The Rev spoke calm and gentle, but his eyes were about to give him up.

Nick sat down and his face went blank. By then we'd all ran out of something, I don't know what. Those four starter sentences were looking down at us.

1. He felt great anguish in his heart.

2. With deep sadness he was pondering the mistakes of his youth.

3. Feather light and quiet as winter snow he takes his leave.

4. Silence or violence, are they the only two responses?

The Rev went on, 'We don't know all the details of how Hamish died, but we will learn

more later in the day. And boys, all the nois
and the yelling today is important. Sometimes
it takes a lot of energy to show that we love
somebody. Being that angry is a sign that you
guys loved Hamish. But we will also have other
ways to show our respect for him.'

Respect. Respect and love. That's what the
Rev reckoned our noise was all about.

And that is how we got the news of Hamish.
The sentences never got anything written
onto them, they just sat there, talking about
somebody who was not there to read them.

They're not starter sentences, are they?
They're ender sentences.

Clem needs some mercy today, that's for sure.

Clem.

TUESDAY, AUGUST 4
HOW HAMISH DIED

Dear Gram

We got told about how Hamish died. He had
a drug overdose and that's the rotten truth. I
never knew he even did drugs but some of the
kids here brag about how they smoke dope and
some of them bring it to school, but mostly it
gets found. But Hamish didn't die from dope,
but from some other rotten stuff.

The reason that they didn't tell us straight up

was that the kid who sold it to him was Bundy and you know what I reckon about him and the Aprilia. Well, they took Bundy away and now he is in some youth remand centre and the coppers are all over him like a rash.

Hamish has a little brother who was also doing drugs but he didn't die. This is so complicated and it's no wonder that we all sat in that class on Monday and started to go crazy.

It is so hard to do anything about Hamish. When I get into session I am always going on about something, but now Hamish has died I sit doing nothing. Saying nothing. And I was too scared to ring up Violet and tell her because her mum and dad might set her off me but I did it anyway and I'm glad I did.

When I rang her up she was upset and she told her mum and dad that a friend of mine had died and they invited me to their place on the weekend if I wanted somewhere to chill out. But it's Hamish who died and they feel sorry for me and that's not right.

Anyway, there's going to be a funeral but I don't know anything about that yet. And you know what? I hardly even know what day it is and I had to ask and it's Tuesday. Monday was yesterday but it feels like Monday is still happening. I think my brain has stopped.

Lunchtime a few of us got out on the bikes

just to ride the short track and Mr O'Neill came along but he didn't do groups or anything, he was just there. Sometimes he canes the track with us but today he was just riding along behind us and we were all caning it and yelling and stuff. I reckon that we probably scared some of the new growth off the trees.

What am I going to do, Gram? I am so poisonous about what happened and how Hamish was at school on Friday and he was not there on Monday and that was that. 'Feather light and quiet as winter snow he takes his leave'.

I'd like to start this week over with a normal Monday and no bad news. Anyway I've got session with the Rev tomorrow and our overnight camps have been cancelled until the funeral. Classes are going on as normal but there is not a lot of normal happening.

Clem.

DVD Review in 100 words

'The Boy With Green Hair'

This is one silly 1950s movie. A boy's parents are killed in World War II. His hair turns green (yep, you read it right) as a sign for world peace. But then not even his mates want him around. A black and white movie with painted in colour, that green hair cracks me up. It's about how people who are different get excluded. There's a school full of different kids here at Rocky valley. War is not the only thing that is bad for children.

WEDNESDAY, AUGUST 5
DEADLY QUIET

Dear Gram

I had session with the Rev today and it was pretty terrible. It's often pretty full-on but today was probably the worst. I sat and he sat waiting for me. Then I would say something and it was so pathetic that I wanted to chase the words out of the air before the Rev heard them. And he didn't say much today. We just sat and looked. I thought it would make me feel better but it didn't, it just made me see how empty I was.

They tell us that the funeral will be on Friday morning and the school will be there and when they take Hamish out of the church we will stand on each side down the stairs. Last night Dad asked me if I wanted him to take me to the funeral or if I wanted to go with school. I told him I wanted him to take me. I was glad Dad offered first coz it would be fully septic having to ask something like that from your own dad. It would be like bumping into his rear wheel for following too closely. So I will see the other boys at the funeral and then I think we've got something happening at the school.

Anyway, that was Wednesday and my time with the Rev, which was pretty terrible, and my time with Dad, which was better than most. It was like the day was back to front or something.

I don't know if Violet is coming to the funeral but I will be with my dad and with the other boys from school. It would be excellent to have her there but I still don't know what she will do. I'm not good at this stuff I reckon and I still haven't cried about Hamish even though I am so fully blistered and upset.

Love from Clem.

FRIDAY, AUGUST 7
AFTER THE FUNERAL THE EMPTY

Dear Gram

The funeral was today and everyone was weird, the kids from school that is. Violet came with her mum and sat with Dad and me and the church was fully packed out and you know what? The Rev was helping to run the funeral. Fully true, there he was. It turns out he's some sort of church dude and I didn't know that. You sure can get these things wrong sometimes I tell you.

Hamish's mum and his brother were all alone and his dad didn't even show up. His brother is in year seven and he was doing drugs with Hamish and these older guys. He's so lucky he didn't die when Hamish did.

When they took Hamish from the church

everyone from school stood down each side of the steps in honour of him. They had his mountain bike in the church coz that was the real Hamish and he loved going flat out so much. Over the coffin they had his bike shirt and helmet but it looked a bit weird among all those flowers.

When I was sitting there with Dad and Violet and her mum it was like I was in a family at last and it felt peculiar. And I looked up at Hamish's mum and his brother and thought, there's another family that's been knocked about fit to destroy. And it was then that I started to cry and I just couldn't stop coz I knew that there was Hamish in that coffin and under the flowers and the mountain bike helmet.

And I cried so hard that Dad put his arm around me and then I saw that Violet was crying too and that shocked me coz she never met Hamish. I suppose that is what families do, and for a little while we were just part of this big Hamish family.

Gram, I don't want to go to another funeral ever. This was so hard but after my crying stopped I managed to feel a bit better and Dad took his arm away and said, 'Are you OK?' And I said, 'Yeah.' And then Violet put her arm around me and it was enough to start me crying all over again but I only did a little bit and I think that was for me and not for Hamish this time.

I can't believe that Hamish is gone with all his moon painting light across the water. I was in the church and stood on those steps and I still can't believe it. But after the funeral we went back to school except Dad went to work and Violet and her mum went home. They had the school bus there to take us back if we wanted to go and we all went back, every one of us, except Hamish and Bundy.

When we got back to school we sat with the teachers and they asked us how we wanted to spend the rest of the day and a couple of guys suggested tackling the track or the ropes and some of the boys said they wanted to go out camping for the night. So we had this choosing thing happening like we do sometimes and we decided to light a fire in the middle of the paddock and we talked about Hamish and how he was always talking about girls and even about the toxic things that he did.

But mostly we talked about his speed and his style and being so agromaniac and reckless when he was racing. Then someone said that he rode his races as if he had a sign across his back that said 'Show No Mercy' and that was when I lost it and started to cry fit to sink.

When I got home Dad was already there as

he left work early so he could be there when I got back from school. That was fully good of him and he asked me how I was doing and how the school had been after the funeral. So I told him how we had the campfire in the daytime and talked about Hamish but I didn't tell him about me crying and the shame in front of everyone.

I told him how I rode home on a school bike and all I could think of was of Hamish straining like mad to stay in front of me, and how it was all I could stand to stop myself from PacManning all the way home like we sometimes do. That's what I told Dad and he was OK with that.

From Clem the Merciful.

SATURDAY, AUGUST 8
FAMILY ZONE

Dear Gram

I think I am going to bust open with all the stuff that is happening. First there was Violet asking if I wanted to go with her. Then the bracelet. Then her mum and dad liking me. Then the Rev's bike buring up and all that trouble. Then Hamish dying and the funeral and what was happening with Bundy. Then Saturday and going over to Violet's house.

We sat in the kitchen with her mum and dad

and drank Coke and they asked me how I was doing and what I had done after the funeral and it was just like with Dad the night before. And I was cheered up by that and feeling a bit better about the sadness and everything coz there was suddenly so many people that cared about what was happening.

Violet's house is much tidier than Dad's house and it is nicer too coz there are people living there and not just coming and going like it is with Dad and me. So we sat around for a while, but with everything that had happened in the last week it was awkward for me to talk too much and Mrs Carter suggested that we have some lunch and then we all go to the movies. Well, Violet and I looked at each other with a bit of a laugh and I went red again when I remembered us kissing. And she could see what I was thinking I reckon and smiled and said with her eyes all sparkly, 'That would be wonderful.'

So that is what we did, except that when we went to find seats her dad had this big grin and he said, 'You two can find seats up there and we will sit down here where you can keep an eye on us.' He is so coolio-funny but I was thinking he's probably got rear view mirrors on his glasses, and Violet was very incredible about it and she said, 'No, let's all sit together,' which shocked me.

And Violet just stopped at one row of seats and she got us to go along the seats so that I was sitting with her on one side and her mum on the other. Violet and me held hands and for the first time ever I sat next to a mum. And that movie went for one hundred and fifteen minutes and that is how many minutes I got to soak it up. I reckon Violet planned it like that coz she is so in the zone. You know, Gram, I get fully confused by families sometimes, I really do.

Love from Clem.

TUESDAY, AUGUST 11
STRAIGHTENING OUT THE REV

Dear Gram

School is trying to get back into gear. We did English again on Monday and Mr German had different sentences up on the board. It still didn't feel right.

After English I went to ask the Rev for a special session. I got to see him today and I asked him straight out about him being like a priest coz I didn't want to have him wrong in my mind about his nickname meaning the rev-head thing. And he told me he is a minister but not working in a church these days.

And I looked at him and said, 'That is the first time you have ever answered a question straight up like that. And he said he answered my question like that because it was not something that I could find out from my own mind.

Then I asked him what the name Paterson means and he said, 'Son of Patrick.' Got that one wrong, but it's a long time ago now.

'Well here's another straight up question, how do I know that there really is a God?'

He said, 'What makes it important for you that there really is a God?'

I had to think about that, and I said, 'What about my mum and my gram who died and what about Hamish? If there is no God and no heaven then I'll never see them again.'

'Do you ever pray about anything, Clem?' he asked.

'How can you talk to somebody you can't see?' I said.

'You write letters to somebody you can't see.' That was a shocker for me to hear.

'Perhaps your questions about God are like those letters,' he said.

I tell you, Gram, the Rev sure knows how to get under your skin, and he did with that comment. Praying is something that I haven't got a clue about, but writing these letters has turned out to be fully easy.

So that serious gangsta car has got nothing to do with his nickname, but he sure makes quick getaways whenever I ask about anything in session, that's for sure.

Clem with love.

WEDNESDAY, AUGUST 12
THAT TEACHER IN YEAR FIVE

Dear Gram

There are some things that I want to talk to the Rev about but I can't seem to get the words out. About that teacher in primary school and what he did. No kid should have to talk or even think about stuff that is so fully straight-up toxic.

I remember when my dad came to school when I was in trouble. That teacher told him my behaviour was not so good and it was because my mum had died and I was like a lost boy. That's how he explained why I was making trouble for everyone.

And Dad and the teacher sat talking about me like that and I could see that Dad wasn't going to believe me and it was bad enough when I told him at home that this teacher did weird stuff and he said, 'He is funny isn't he?' And that isn't what I meant but when the teacher told my dad why my behaviour wasn't so good and Dad believed him, well I knew then that nobody was going to believe me about that teacher.

That is what I want to say to the Rev but I can't talk about those things with anybody and that's the sad truth of it.

Clem.

FRIDAY, AUGUST 14
ULTRA SCIENCE EXPERIMENT

Dear Gram

We've been doing this mad science class with Mr Williams and he is the craziest teacher on the high ropes when he gets going. And this is the thing in science. If you get this stuff called sodium hydroxide on you it will destroy where it touches just like that, coz sodium reacts to everything at the touch of a button or even a sideways glance.

We have people like that at this school and you can touch their button just by a glance and they go fully carcino-lethal. I've got the bruises to prove it. Bundy was one of those people. Brian is another, but we don't much set him off so much now that he is more of a friend.

Well, this sodium hydroxide even makes water boil and that is the truth. You put some into the water and it will boil all by itself. And you have to always put the powder into the water and not the other way around coz that is even more dangerous.

Mr Williams put on this old rock CD with a song called 'Smoke on the Water' to remind us to slowly sprinkle the sodium hydroxide on the water to make it boil. He must be a bit of a rock star tragic from way back. So there we were doing this coolio experiment with Mr Williams' old rock music going in the background, and that is another reason why Rocky Valley really rocks.

We had this water heating up, but as slowly as we could so it didn't blast all that sodium over us, which would take our skin off. Mr Williams had some normal olive oil, and we each measured how much we needed. We slowly poured the water into the oil and stirred it around. And what happened then was so fully straight-up that not even Jacko said anything funny.

The water with the sodium just mixed straight into that oil and it started to go milky misty and to thicken up. We slowly stirred the stuff until it was thick as custard which is called Trace, coz you can leave traces of the spoon across the top, and that whole process of it getting thicker while you mix it is called saponification which is the only clue that I will give you.

Mr Williams showed us some that he did before and it had gone hard by then and you know what it was? It was soap! No kidding, this is straight-up. We poured our stuff into little pans so it can harden and dry out for a month which is called the curing process.

I tell you Gram it's really freaky when you think of that sodium hydroxide which can take your skin off and here it is after we slowly got the heat out of it in the water and mixed it into that olive oil.

I've got an idea about this science class and that idea involves Mr O'Neill who does groups. And I bet in group this week Mr O'Neill will get us talking about how some of us react to things, like Brian the Brain does so easily and

Bundy used to react like superflak when he was here but now that position's been taken by Nick. That's what I bet will happen in group this week and that is because in this school they are mega-tricky about things like this and I am learning to get it ahead of time.

You know what I would like? I would like to stop reacting full-on like sodium hydroxide fit to take your skin off. But somebody has to slowly get the heat out and then wait for the curing process to happen. That's what I would like. For Nick, and for Brian, and for me.

Love from Clem the Clean.

Bike Review in 100 Words

Aprilia Pegaso 650 Trail

The Rev turned up with a new
Aprilia The Pegaso is a road/trail
crossover style. And style is the only
word for this Italian beauty. Red
and black, pretty as the 1000R but
catwoman hardcore, complete with
a snarty lion on the side. 650cc single
cylinder engine, long travel suspension
for dirt roads. Pillion seat has no
cover, I guess that's still important.
This is my kind of motorbike.

TUESDAY, AUGUST 18
THE BIRTHDAY, THE BIKE SHOP, THE BEER

Dear Gram

Told Dad about the soap and how some people are sodium hydroxide and react fit to take your skin off and he was surprised that we did all that in school. He never did that stuff and never learned that it was called saponification and it felt the best to be able to tell him about that. And then I asked him about a new mountain bike that has full shockers and hydraulic disc brakes and he was so up there about that and asked if I could wait for my birthday which is not that far away.

So that is how our conversation went and I wanted us to go straight down to the bike shop and look through the window coz it was night and he said that we could do that on the weekend. And now I can't wait until the weekend and until my birthday but I am OK about that coz Dad was so full-on listening.

He was kind of quiet when we were speaking and not taking too much of the talk for himself and I wondered if he had something on his mind.

I wondered if Dad was worried about Lyndel coz he hasn't even mentioned her name for ages but I was nervous about that. Then I remembered that the silence is not my friend, coz the silence will only do what the silence always does, which is mostly nothing. It especially won't ask Dad my question so I asked him if he was worried about Lyndal or something.

And he said, 'No, I am worried about what happened to Hamish.' And that was a full-on shock to me coz he never even met Hamish.

I didn't know how to react to that coz some of the sodium hydroxide in me has been cooled off since I got to this school, but it made me sad to be thinking about Hamish again. And then Dad said that he would be really worried if I was to be doing drugs and that was what he was mostly worried about and why he wasn't saying much.

I felt good about telling him that I hadn't done drugs ever, not even the dope that some boys try to bring to school. Then I got to telling him that some kids from my old school and me. Sometimes we got slabs of beer to drink in another boy's house coz his dad was always away working.

It sounded like maybe I was talking about Dad always being away but it hasn't been like that so much for a while now. Dad asked if I liked the beer and I said not much and he was pleased about that I think. And I full-on don't coz I see him when he drinks beer, which is usually when he breaks up with a girlfriend, and he doesn't look like I want to be looking if you get what I mean.

And that was our conversation about drugs and beer.

Dad was pretty quiet after that and I thought he was sad for Hamish. Maybe he was thinking, what if it had been Clem instead of Hamish? And that's what I would have thought, too.

After we had that talk about Hamish and drugs and beer I rang Violet. She wasn't home and I spoke to her mum instead and she asked me how I had been and how the other boys at the school were and I knew what she meant and neither of us had to say Hamish's name. And I asked her to tell Violet about what Dad said about the mountain bike for my birthday and would she like to come to the bike shop on Saturday and look around. And Mrs Carter was coolio-froolio with that and would tell Violet.

I said, 'Thanks, you are really ultra like Violet is,' and she laughed over the phone with me. Suddenly I said, 'Mrs Carter, why does Violet like me?'

Mrs Carter said, 'Clem, it is easy to like you.'

And I said, 'But I've been in trouble and get mad at so much stuff and Violet is not like that at all.'

Mrs Carter said, 'Clem, Violet was always

the first to go dancing in the rain.' And that stopped me right there and I said, 'I don't get it.' Then she said, 'Some people go dancing in the rain, others just get wet.'

I am going to have to think about that. But I still don't get it.

Maybe I do get it.

Love from Clem.

WEDNESDAY, AUGUST 19
BEING MR PATERSON

Dear Gram

You won't believe this but two amazing things have happened in two days. Mostly if the same thing happens two days running it means I've got bruises from two different fights but these two things are madaz different. Last night I had that radicool conversation with Dad about everything and today it was with Mr Paterson who is really the Rev but today he wasn't.

I was out at the paddock and talking to the calf and leaning on the fence and the Rev walked up and said, 'G'day Clem.'

So I said, 'G'day Rev.' He leaned against the fence beside me and we both just looked out over the paddock. I was still scritching the calf. And then I blurted out, 'Can you be Mr Paterson for a bit instead of being the Rev?'

He said, 'How do you mean, Clem?'

I was nervous by this time. 'Can you just answer some questions for me without doing that slippery thing like you do in sessions?'

'Do you think I'm being slippery in sessions?'

'When I ask a question mostly you just lay it back onto me somehow and I don't want you to do that out here with the calf and all.'

I thought saying about the calf there sounded a bit stupid but the Rev mustn't have coz he didn't say anything about the calf comment. He reached over the fence and gave the calf a scritch. Then he said, 'Can you give me an example?'

Well I nearly went off coz it sounded like he'd just done the slippery thing on me again there, but I held it. I said to him, 'Like that time I saw you in town with all those kids in the car and you just said, 'Tell me what you were thinking when you saw us drive past'. How come you didn't tell me who those kids were when one of them was Emily?'

'I remember that. But your question, about who was in the car with me, that was not the real question. The real question was hidden away somewhere.'

And I was like, 'What's the go with that?'

'Clem, you asked me about who was in the car with me, but the real question concerned your dad and a motorbike.'

'I don't get it. That is full-on weird.'

We had to talk for ages before I got it and it's still a bit tricky for me but I know he wasn't being slippery. It's those metaphors again. Sometimes we have a question that hurts too much to come to the surface. We keep finding metaphors but the metaphor questions don't work. One day the real question comes up and finds the real answer. Or something.

'I think my metaphor question was about who was in the car with you, but the real question was, 'How come my dad doesn't have room for me?'

'That sounds right. The dad question inside you saw me being a dad and recognised its metaphor. The metaphor helped the real question come to the surface.'

I turned around to face him more straight on. 'Mr Paterson, do you have any other kids apart from Emily?'

'I have three children and you met Emily who is eight. There are twin boys called Simon and Peter and they are ten, and you saw my wife in the car that day too, and her name is Marilyn. How about that for a full answer?'

'That is madaz of you to tell me all that.'

'Clem, if I told you the names of my family way back when you asked about them, do you think it would have answered your real question?'

'I would still be toxic about my dad wouldn't I?'

'Yes, you probably would.'

We stayed like that for a bit. A couple of farmers looking out over the paddock. Waiting for better weather.

'Mr Paterson, why doesn't my dad stick to me?'

'I don't know for sure but let's have a go. Imagine a man and his wife are very much in love. They have a new baby. Suddenly the wife is gone. The man wants to chase after her but the baby is crying and needs him. He looks one way into what used to be and he looks the other way into the eyes of his newborn son. How can he choose between those two?'

'That fully sucks that somebody has to choose like that!' I got all red-mist on this one and that is when the calf suddenly skits off, coz he's skitty sometimes and he's been standing there while we scritched his head all the way up to now. I suppose he just couldn't take me getting toxic but seeing him get nervous slowed me down a bit.

Change of subject time suddenly arrived so I said, 'Do you think the calf should have a name?'

'I think of him as Mr Bojangles,' the Rev said.

'What does that mean?'

'There's a famous old song about a dancer who was light on his feet. The calf reminds me of it. That's all, nothing too serious.'

'Hamish was light on his feet,' I said.

'He sure was.' The Rev smiled.

We leaned against the fence a bit longer, but the conversation was over. 'You can go back to being the Rev if you want to,' I said. We both smiled at that. Sometimes I get it.

I'm not so toxic on Dad now that I understand a bit, especially about my guess last night that he was saying to himself, 'What if it was Clem and not Hamish?' Coz if I am right on that guess then it means he is a bit stuck on me after all.

I hope so.

Love from Clem.

Recipe For Disaster

Sorting it with Brian

Brian and me have come up with
something that beats cling wrap
on the toilet bowl.
Dissolve lemon/lime jelly crystals in
hot water. Pour into toilet
bowl late at night. Choose which
toilet very carefully.
We call this Stopping the Brain Drain.

MONDAY, AUGUST 24
NICK & ME

Dear Gram

You know about Nick and how he gets toxic. Well, he doesn't like being passed on the track, but that happens if you are not fast enough. Our worst ever day was when I said, 'Nick is not a slow racer, and Nick is not a fast racer. Nick is a half-fast racer.' Everybody laughed. Except Nick. I should have known there would be bruises for me in that joke. No pain, no gain.

Today we were riding the track and there were about ten of us there with Mr Sykes who is a bit big to fit properly on a mountain bike but he does OK.

If it is not a race sometimes we fool around and we try to knock each other off by tracking the next person's back wheel with our front wheel. That can be fun but you have to be careful coz you only want the other guy to fall off and not run over him and fall off yourself.

Sometimes we end up with a buckle in a wheel and Mr Sykes stands on the wheel and pulls it back to shape enough for us to ride some more. Then we have to fix it properly back at the school with a little spanner on the spokes but most of us can't get that right. And it's Mr Hartley who teaches us about that spanner on the spokes and that is full-on funny coz it was him who taught us about tracking in the first place. I reckon Mr Hartley is sixteen in his head, but he looks like sixty from the outside. There's some full-on fierce buckled wheels back at the school sometimes and that is really nangtastic coz it means there has been some hot tracking.

Getting close to the gully today, where I'm always serious, I passed Nick and he tried to track me for payback and I had to duck and weave. So I slowed up a bit and let him have it in both ears.

'Nick Off!' I yelled, coz saying that presses his button and he goes ape. I knew there were going to be bruises in this one coz he gets up beside me and yells out, 'Who are you bagging out, stick insect?' That's what I get sometimes for being skinny. And as soon as he yells that he steers straight into my front wheel and we both hit the dirt, luckily before we got too steep down into the gully.

He was on top of me like a shot with his fists and was madaz agroholic but I wasn't going to back down on that one, no way, coz that would be the end of me, so I was back into him with my fists. Suddenly Mr Sykes comes out of nowhere and he lifts us up with a hand on each and holds us apart and that man is like a giant when he does that. And having Mr Sykes on the spot so quick is exactly what we didn't want because we try to keep our fights secret from the teachers otherwise we get really scarfed up.

And we keep our bruises secret too, especially from the boy who hit us, which is a really full-on rule for us otherwise we would not be able to take the shame.

Anyway, Mr Sykes was holding us apart and all the other boys were there by now and they all love a fight when it is somebody else. Mr Sykes gets really hot when there is fisties on the track. 'Are you two in the same group?' and we say, 'No.' And he says, 'It might be time we got you both together. I'll see Mr O'Neill about that.'

Well then Nick and I looked at each other and we both hated that idea and by then I was feeling the bruises on my ribs and I was hoping he had some bruises too. But Nick can't hit like Bundy used to and I know that for sure.

In my old school I would get into fights and get warnings and no matter how quickly us kids made up those warnings would stay and when there is enough warnings I would get suspended. Here they do things differently but I've never heard of them putting two boys into the same group for something like this.

And the more I write about this thing the more I get worked up coz what Nick did is so black and white wrong, but I know that if

I try to talk about how wrong it was I will get something like, 'It might not be so black and white, you know.' We get that around here. 'Things are not always so black and white.'

Why don't I see it? I just have to add in a few shades of grey and Nick is not so much of a zit-head. As if.

It's a bit funny considering that on live-ins they keep showing black and white DVDs of boys in trouble, like that one about 'Lord of the Flies' where they were so tribal they started killing each other. I dunno where they get those DVDs. Maybe there's a black and white warehouse somewhere up behind the Shack.

What would they know about black and white anyway? That's what I want to know. I am so revved up and it's all Nick's fault for what he did in tracking my front wheel which is black and white against the rules. Nick needs to see a little black and blue, that's what he needs. Now I am waiting for Mr O'Neill to tell us what is going to happen.

I remain your obedient servant.

We learned in English that people used to end letters like that but did they mean it in person? Not.

Clem.

WEDNESDAY, AUGUST 26
DNA

Dear Gram

Jacko set up Mr Williams something brilliant and he was stand-up funny. Mr Williams was doing yada-yada-yada stuff, he is such a yadaholic, and he said, 'A tower subtends an angle of fifteen degrees at a distance of two hundred metres,' and it's trigonometry. But the numbers don't sit straight with me. Trigonometry is about measuring triangles. I get the word but I can't get the numbers.

And anyway Mr Williams was trying to get me to get it right and there were other boys who weren't getting either it but Mr Williams is mostly chilled about that. Not like teachers I had in normal school.

And then Jacko said, 'Mr Williams, you shouldn't be too tough on these boys because they are all members of the DNA, which is the National Dyslexics Association.'

Mr Williams looked up puzzled and I could tell he didn't quite get it but Jacko and I sat there laughing fit to bust ourselves.

Then Jacko said, 'The DNA, sir. Putting the sex back in dyslexia.'

That really got me going and by then Mr Williams had got it and he laughed like crazy but some of the other kids sat there saying, 'What?'

Nothing yet from Mr O'Neill about Nick and me, but I am patient and the bruises are coloured up.

Love from Colourful Clem. Ha ha, I am still laughing about the DNA joke.

DVD Review in 100 words
'The 400 Blows'

A French DVD with English subtitles, but a meaningless title. This boy keeps getting into trouble but it's not really his fault. His mother doesn't want him and she gets a judge to put him in a detention centre but he runs away.

The DVD ends with him coming to the ocean and there's nowhere else for him to run. He turns to look back at where he came from but back there not even his mother wants him.

That sucks I reckon.

Did I mention it was black and white?

FRIDAY, AUGUST 28
LIKE TRIGONOMETRY

Dear Gram

Mr O'Neill got Nick and me together in his office and we were looking at each other sideways and that was it for us. And he said, 'OK guys, we're off to do some stuff.' And you know what we did? He took us to the high ropes course.

When we got to the ropes Mr O'Neill said we had to choose who was going to belay the other first. And that was tough for me coz I wanted to belay Nick and then just let him drop. Mr O'Neill said we could take whatever time it took to make our decision and he just stood there with us near the rope ladder but neither of us spoke.

And I remembered that the silence is not my friend and so I decided to make the decision for us.

'I will belay Nick first,' I said, and I was final with that.

Mr O'Neill said to Nick, 'What do you think of that suggestion?'

'What if he drops me on purpose?'

'If you have a different suggestion we can hear them both and you two can decide between them.'

Nick said to me, 'Are you thinking about dropping me?'

'I was thinking that at first,' I said, 'but I will belay you properly.' Nick thought about that. 'OK,' he said.

Mr O'Neill sent Nick up into the ropes and said, 'Today you will jump off deliberately and Clem will hold you.'

We both looked at him and at each other. And then Nick jumped. I held him easy, but it was full-on weird when I had to trust Nick to hold me.

Mr O'Neill said, 'OK guys, this time you will be up there together on different tracks. I want to see some speed and we are going to do a rope race.' I had never heard of a rope race.

Mr O'Neill had this trick of handling two belay ropes at once and we started running. Nick can get along those ropes faster than I can, but I wasn't about to let him bruise me in a fight and then outrun me in a race. He won every time and I wasn't OK with that but I figured I would get him later with something.

You can't run the ropes for too long because the rope starts to ache your feet and we finished up and headed back. Mr O'Neill said he would see us on Monday and each of us will tell the story about our fight from our own angle. It's a bit like trigonometry, which I am not the best at.

Love from Clem.

SATURDAY, AUGUST 29
TAGGIN' THE SCREAMIN' DEMON

Dear Gram

Saturday morning I was up early to get to Ted's bike shop. Dad was dragging the chain full-on and we got to the shop and it wasn't even opened yet, but I was hot to trot. Mr Carter dropped Violet at the shop and she looked amazing and she was wearing the bracelet.

I said, 'Haven't you taken that off yet?' and she whispered to me she even wears it in the shower and I went off to Mars on that and got redder and redder. Dad said to me, 'Are you OK?' And Violet just grinned coz she knew what I was thinking. It's not easy being a kinesthetic, but there was definitely a big dose of visual in me when she said that I tell you. Sometimes when she hugs me it's as if I'm about to explode off the planet, but it's better not to think too much of that when I'm standing in front of a bike shop with Dad.

Ted came and opened up and Dad said my birthday was coming up and we just wanted to see what he had in there. Those bikes are fully serious and there was nothing like mine there which is a bit old and is not tricked out or anything. Dad said for Violet and me to look around while he talked with Ted.

I was in the zone with all those bikes. There were rear shockers everywhere and hydraulic disc brakes and XTR shifters and carbon fibre handlebars, and I was like, 'Where do I look next?' And I tried to think of how long until my birthday.

Dad and Ted had talked about money and Ted told me, 'The bikes in this section would fit into that range,' and I hadn't even looked at the price tags but when I did it was more than I could think about even on 'Deal or No Deal'. We were standing near a Bianchi like the Rev has, and that was a shocker to me I can tell you. Dad is being red hot with money for this bike.

Violet and I looked all through that section again and I picked out a bike that was a hot purple colour coz of Violet and it is called a Screamin' Demon which is the most fantastic name. And the bike has fantastic Rock Shocks and hydraulic disc brakes and XTR RapidFires and twenty-seven gears and a madaz lightweight frame that came straight from outer space. But that price tag shocked me and I thought OK of Dad about that.

Ted said he would tag the bike and put it out the back for me and he got me to write my name on the tag. I nearly can't believe I have to wait till my birthday to get onto that Screamin' Demon.

Mr Carter met us at the smoothie bar with me buzzing and grinning and I couldn't hardly stand still. I wanted to pay for the smoothies and hoped that I had enough pocket money even if I didn't get to take Violet to the movies. And Dad and Mr Carter let me pay even though it took most of my money.

And that is when Mr Carter said he hoped the boys at the school were doing OK since the funeral for Hamish and I went really quiet when he said that. Then he said he was sorry that I had lost a friend who kept me on my toes when we were racing. I was thinking for a bit and I told him, 'Thank you.'

Then he said something seriously full-on. He said he hoped that there was another boy at the school who could give me as much competition as Hamish did and keep me running hard on that new bike. And I said, 'I hope so, too.' And so it was suddenly serious talk at the smoothie bar.

All that good stuff on Saturday and Mr O'Neill is going to sort out Nick and me on Monday morning. It's like the universe is giving me a reality check.

Love from Clem.

MONDAY, AUGUST 31
NICK AND ME AND DEFINITE DANGER

Dear Gram

Things are getting thick and fast around here. Mr O'Neill saw Nick and me today. We were looking sideways between us again and we didn't know what Mr O'Neill was going to do but we just sat down in his office.

Mr O'Neill said that he was going to make this as simple as possible but no simpler. He told us that the answer to our fight was somewhere in us and we could share that answer between us if we were tough enough. And that was a straight-up shock because Nick had already tracked my front wheel and given me bruises and beat me on the rope races and it was not fair that we should have to see who was the toughest with me being so skinny and already with bruises.

And that is what I said straight up to Mr O'Neill and he accepted that and then he asked Nick, 'What do you think about what Clem has just said?' And Nick was smiling a bit and said he didn't mind what Mr O'Neill suggested. And I could see that there were more bruises coming up but I wasn't going to back down I can tell you.

So Mr O'Neill said to Nick, 'Would you like

to go first at meeting the challenge that I will set for both of you?' and Nick said, 'OK.' And I was thinking that Mr O'Neill would set more stuff like on the ropes but no way. What he did was beyond anything.

Mr O'Neill said, 'Nick, you are a tough kind of kid. Are you tough enough to tell Clem truthfully why you don't like it when someone says, "Nick off" to you like he did?' And Nick just sat there and went blank in his eyes and his face went white and I've never seen anyone go like that ever. And Mr O'Neill sat and waited and I sat and stared coz Nick was going someplace in his head that I don't know of and his eyes were like stones and I swear he couldn't even see out of them.

Then Nick started to cry and that is seriously hard for anyone around here, but especially for someone as tough as Nick. He just sat in that chair and didn't move except those tears coming from his eyes and it kept on going for ages. Then Mr O'Neill said to him, 'Nick, can you meet the challenge or is it too tough for you?' And that is when Nick started to look out of his eyes again and I was pleased about that even if Nick is so toxic.

And Nick said, 'I will tell him,' and Mr O'Neill said, 'Nick, I'm glad you can accept the challenge. Is there anything I can do to help you?' And Nick said 'No.' Then he started to talk.

He talked about his father who has picked on him and bashed him all his life. His father hits him with beer bottles or BBQ tongs or whatever is in his hand at the time and says to him, 'Nick off,' and laughs as if he has cracked a joke, but he hasn't really. And he said that his father has done that for his whole life and now Nick is taller and bigger than his father, but he still keeps doing it coz he knows Nick is scared of him as if he is still a little kid.

And that is the story of Nick and why he gets so toxic when anyone says that to him. And that is why he was so agroholic on me that day. All because of his father. And Nick looked at me as he said every word and that is full-on hard to do I reckon and I respect him for that straight-up.

And then Mr O'Neill asked me if there was any response I wanted to make to Nick. So I told Nick I was sorry for calling him that name when I knew it would set him off, but I was angry at him tracking my wheel at the top of the gully. I would not set him off like that again now that I knew about his dad. And I said that I was sorry his dad was like that because dads should stick to their sons and not treat them like crap. And then I said that I respected him for telling me the story when it made him cry in front of me.

Then Mr O'Neill said, 'Nick, do you accept Clem's response?' And Nick said, 'Thanks Clem,' which is not anything like I was expecting when we started this session.

Then Mr O'Neill said to me, 'Clem, I've got a challenge for you too if you're tough enough.' Suddenly I got nervous coz I had seen how tough it had been for Nick but I knew I was in the right and I said, 'OK.'

Mr O'Neill said, 'Clem, can you tell Nick truthfully why you have worked at it over many years to make life so hard for your dad?' And I was high-level shocked about what he just said coz it was my dad that made life hard for me.

I just sat there and things went through my mind like the times he yelled me out and said it was my fault that my mum died, and how he was like a motorbike with no room for a passenger. And it was not fair what Mr O'Neill had said about me making life hard for him. And I didn't know what was worse, having all that running inside me all my life or Mr O'Neill being so unfair, and I could feel my eyes heating up inside.

I was about to tell Nick that Mr O'Neill got it wrong but I remembered that Dad said he worried I might be doing drugs and about,

'What if it was Clem instead of Hamish?' I was getting hyperdrive but my mouth would not give me any words and it was like Clem the Clam was back but his engine was roaring. And then I looked at Mr O'Neill and was about to tell him he had it wrong but this was the test of toughness and Nick had taken it up and now it was my turn.

Mr O'Neill said, 'Clem, can you meet the challenge or is it too tough for you?' And I thought this was a bad time to give up and I remembered how Nick had those eyes like stones and I wondered if that is what I was like to him. And I said, 'I will tell him.'

Mr O'Neill said, 'Clem, I'm glad you can accept the challenge. Is there anything I can do to help you?' And I said, 'No.'

So I told Nick that my mum had died as I was being born and it was like someone came along to Dad and took away his wife who he loved like crazy and dropped this baby there instead. And Dad had to be both dad and mum, which was impossible for anyone.

I told him how I grew up hurting and angry and Dad copped all my crap and I started making trouble at school and they had to call Dad in from work so he would take more notice of me. And I told Nick of how being suspended from school was the greatest buzz and Dad didn't know what to do about it.

Then Dad got a job that took him away a lot so he could leave me with my gram. But Gram got sick and died and it was like the world came to an end. Dad had to have me home all the time.

I figured out that I could really stir Dad up by getting into trouble with the police. That was something he never knew how to handle and life became harder and harder for both of us. It was like winning a major battle in a war that would never end.

And I told Nick that even though I blamed my dad for not sticking to me and for being like a motorbike without room for a passenger, he was really worried about me all the time but I wouldn't ever let him show it and now that I was at this school I was only just starting to see that my dad wanted all that time to stick with me but I wouldn't let him.

I turned my anger on everybody since I was a little kid, but Dad had taken most of it. And that day on the track I turned my anger on Nick.

It turns out Mr O'Neill was right about me after all. I hated what he said in the beginning but by the time I had said all that to Nick I was feeling a bit different about Mr O'Neill.

Mr O'Neill said, 'Nick, is there any response

you would like to make to what Clem has just said?' And Nick said that he didn't know all that and was sorry about my mum dying. But when I said about all the ways I tried to make life hard for my dad, well that made him think about his dad. And he reckoned it must have been hard for me to admit that all those things were my fault and he respected me for that.

Then Mr O'Neill said, 'You guys are very tough to accept those challenges and I respect you both for how you handled them.' Nick and I just looked at each other.

He told us that when something important like this happens he has the duty to tell the other teachers, but they will not say anything about it to embarrass us, and we should observe the normal group rule of confidentiality and not say anything to anyone of what the other person said.

He asked us how we were feeling about what we had said and we both said, 'OK,' but I know I said some stuff that took me by surprise and I was still in shock a bit. And Mr O'Neill told Nick and me that if we wanted to meet again he would be happy to give us some time, but if we wanted to talk anything through in private then he suggested we see the Rev.

Then he said, 'Is there anything that you would like to do now? You might feel a bit overloaded to go back to class.' We said we didn't know. And that is when he suggested we go with him to check the sheep, who are a bit stupid for me, and the calf who I like, and we checked the chooks for eggs. We didn't talk much.

When we got back it was lunchtime and noisy but we were quiet. Everyone always wants to know what happened when someone gets scarfed up by the teachers. But Nick and I were pretty chilled, which sounds better than it really was, and we didn't say anything.

This is the busiest day of my whole life and the only day that I ever told the proper truth and I am a bit normalised about that now but I am still in shock about it having happened and about what I said to Nick.

Clem.

STILL MONDAY, STILL WRITING

Dear Gram

This is the second letter today. We've got camp this week, which I like. I'm a bit scared about what to say to Dad after telling Nick the truth at last. Campfire makes things easier to say on camp but I don't know how to say serious stuff to Dad.

This letter is to write something about Violet so you know why she is so fantastic for me. She has my photo on her mobile. And me too, of course with her photo. But it sure feels good that she wants me on her mobile.

Violet has a friend named Zoe and they text each other all the time and sometimes I say, 'Show me,' and Violet giggles and says, 'No I can't show you.' And you know what? Sometimes she goes a bit red. I like it when she goes a bit red. Her eyes shine a bit differently and it makes her look even prettier.

I have this idea about them – Violet texts Zoe with, 'I thnk yr bf is a qt esp wn he :),' and Zoe texts back to Violet with 'I thnk yr bf is a qt esp wn he says ur Ultra.'

Well the thing with this is that Zoe is a name that means LIFE and I have put that in capitals. I have a girlfriend who is friends with LIFE and that is so excellent because I didn't think LIFE could ever be my friend. Things are changing for me.

H&K LUL — Which is full-on true.

OXO

Clem.

DvDream Review in 100 words

'The Dream of the Road'

I had a dream of standing on a road that stretched into the distance. I turned around and it stretched into the distance the other way. I could see that one direction went into the past and the other direction into the future. And the road is life. When I woke up I had a new thing in my head. It doesn't matter how far you are along the road of life. What matters is what direction you are heading.

TUESDAY, SEPTEMBER 1
GETTING TRIGONOMETRY

Dear Gram

This is a letter about trigonometry which you know I am not much good at.

The thing about trigonometry is that it only works when there is one angle in that triangle which is straight up. That right angle controls the two other angles which are always sharp and dangerous if you get what I mean.

I have found that when there are two people and they are sharp and dangerous on each other and there is another person who is straight up in himself then those three can work it out. But the person who is straight up is the one who should control the other two.

And that is what Mr O'Neill did with Nick and me. Very sharp of him. But it sure put industrial level danger on me at the time.

Triple love from Clem.

WEDNESDAY, SEPTEMBER 2
THE DAY OF THE DOORBELL

Dear Gram

This is a weird campfire story from camp. Mike, who is Mr O'Neill, told this story about a guy and his wife sitting at home when the doorbell rang. At the door was a stranger with something in his hand.

The stranger said, 'I am leaving this with you for one week. If you press the button you will get one million dollars and someone you don't know will die.' Then he was gone. Those people were full-on freaked out by that bloke. And there on the table was a doorbell button, just like at their front door.

They looked at it and thought about that million dollars. And they started talking about how people died from being sick or accidents or getting old and they asked each other, 'What if it is someone who is going to die anyway?'

They didn't know what to do.

So the doorbell button sat there all week and soon the stranger would be back. Eventually they couldn't take it any more so they jumped in together and pressed the button and at that very moment their doorbell rang. There stood the stranger with a briefcase. He counted out one million dollars.

'Does this mean that someone died?' they asked.

'It was someone you didn't know,' said the stranger as he picked up the doorbell.

'What are you going to do now?' they said as he walked out the door.

'Oh, don't worry. I'll be sure to give this to someone who doesn't know you.'

Suddenly it was a Values for Life class, which was very tricky of Mike to do at the campfire. We were very quiet and just looked into the fire.

Brian almost whispered, 'That is what happened to Hamish.'

I tell you Gram you could have heard the birds snoring in the trees when he said that.

Someone said, 'But Bundy and Hamish knew each other so that doesn't count.'

Then Mike said to Brian, 'You can see it, Brian, can't you?'

And Brian was real quiet and said, 'Yes, I can see it.'

But the rest of us couldn't see it, whatever it was. And to top it off there was Mike telling us all that Brian had got it right for once and we didn't even know what the question was. I don't like it when it turns out like that.

I spent the night dreaming about a doorbell sitting on a table the day I was born. And wondering who pressed the button.

Clem.

THURSDAY, SEPTEMBER 3
THE IDEA AT THE END OF THE UNIVERSE

Dear Gram

I had an idea about how to talk to Dad. We were sitting around the campfire and one of the kids told us about how his aunty has a campfire in her backyard. That sounded pretty odd but he said they sit out there instead of inside so they can look at the stars. His aunty says the stars are like family. The bright stars are for relatives who have recently died and the dimmer stars are for ancestors who died long ago.

I wondered if there is a star up there for my mum. I didn't realise that I said it out loud until somebody said, 'A star for your mum?' And I said kind of quiet, 'My mum died when I was being born.'

This kid said, 'My mum died, too.' I could see his eyes in the firelight and they were kind of glistening. We knew that we were like brothers, which is something the campfire does. And that is what gave me the idea about talking to Dad.

When I got home there was a note from Dad saying that he had to go for a work thing because of new products in his company, which makes the super-tuff Kevlar they put in bullet-proof army jackets and chainsaw trousers and even bomb-disposal clothes. I wish I was wearing some Kevlar when Nick did that bruise on my ribs I can tell you.

Dad said he would be away until Friday to get customers for these new products. And now it is Thursday night and I am writing this instead of talking to Dad and that is OK by me coz I have an idea for tomorrow night and Dad will freak out, but in a good way I hope.

Love Clem.

SUNDAY, SEPTEMBER 6

Dear Gram

I got home in a good mood about what I was going to say to Dad. And Dad was glad to see me in such a good mood and I was glad to see him.

This was the first time I had seen Dad since I told Nick the truth on Monday. And I said to Dad, 'Can we do something that I have an idea about?' And he said, 'What is that?' And I said, 'It would be good to have a talk around a campfire, but we need to build a campfire in the backyard first.' He grinned a bit and said, 'OK.' So we got some branches and stuff that he had pruned off a tree ages ago and did it.

I told Dad how I got angry at Nick, but really I was angry at the whole world. I told Dad that I had taken that anger out on him forever. I told him that I got a real buzz from being suspended from school because it made him take notice of me. And I told him that for a long time there I reckoned he didn't want to stick to me like a father should stick to his son.

This was the first time in my life I ever told him the straight-up honest truth and how sorry I was for making life so hard for him. I could see his eyes in the firelight and they were glistening and I knew then that we could really be Dad and Son.

So that's how the campfire did its thing in our own backyard. Dad said it took strength to say that and that he respected me for everything I said sitting there. He could see that we did love each other and he agreed that it's not easy sometimes. We were quiet again until he said we should get some sleep and I was up with that. I was tired out from walking in the bush and the campfire and the thing with Nick, which was still putting me in shock from it having happened.

Violet rang on Saturday morning but I was still asleep. She asked if I was OK coz my voice sounded different and I told her that I had some serious stuff happening with Dad and I would tell her later at the smoothie bar. And suddenly I was hungry for toast.

Dad appeared and said he'd thought a lot

about last night and it was good to remember what I had said. Then he said he's got something he wanted to do down the street with me. We headed off in the car and he pulled up at the bike shop and asked if I minded having to ride the bike home. And I got ultra-excited but said it's not my birthday yet, and he said he wanted me to have the bike early.

Ted got the bike out of the back and I was like, 'Totally awesome!' when I saw him take that tag off it that had my name in big letters. And Ted gave me a lock and cable so I could lock the bike up before going into the plaza to meet Violet at the smoothie bar and then he loaned me a stack hat so I could ride it out of the shop.

When the bike got into the sun there was another shock waiting for me. That purple bike suddenly turned red on one side when the sun hit sideways on it. That was straight-up steroidacious and I didn't see that trick of the paint inside the shop. This bike is from both ends of the spectrum and fully wicked I can tell you. I got to the smoothie bar very quick to see Violet and tell her about this new surprise.

I couldn't stay in the plaza, though, for being fidgety and we went out to the bike and to the park and I rode that Screamin' Demon all over and I was doing bunny hops and wheelies and even stoppies just in front of Violet and she laughed all the time I was fooling around.

She got a bit quiet when I told her what had happened with me and Dad the night before, and her eyes got glistening and I had to stop talking for a while there. And Violet reached out and she held on to my hand and she said I was totally awesome but she already knew that on our first day in the smoothie bar. That is the solid truth of what she said.

I had a happy heart that day I can tell you but I hope I never have another week that is so busy for my head. Mostly I am glad Dad and I look like getting along as we should, coz it has taken a long time.

Love from Clem.

WEDNESDAY, SEPTEMBER 9
INTO FREEFALL

Dear Gram

School sure has taken it out of me this week and that is the truth. We didn't have a camp this week but we had races and I had my new bike at school and it was totally awesome.

Most of the week was very normal and I was glad that not very much happened because I was so tired in my head. When I had session with the Rev it was a quiet time and I told him about what happened with Nick and with Mr Sykes and Mr O'Neill and he was normal about that and he didn't try any slippery sentences on me and I was surprised about that and relaxed that day.

Then I remembered that Mr O'Neill probably told him already about Nick and me but he wouldn't have heard about Dad and me on the Friday night. I liked telling the Rev about Friday night and how I told Dad that once I thought he was like a motorbike without room for a passenger but I didn't think that any more. The Rev smiled and I relaxed. I must have been pretty relaxed and dropped my guard, coz suddenly I was saying stuff that just came from somewhere underneath.

'When I was in primary school my teacher did things that no teacher should ever do to any kid. I'd hardly started in year five and he wanted to take my clothes off and I knew I was in big trouble.'

And when I said that the whole thing bust out of me.

'That teacher even got my dad to believe that I was bad and could not be trusted to tell the truth. Nobody believed me about anything and it was that man who did that to me.'

I was up on my feet and charging around in the Rev's office like in the old days. I wanted to pick things up off his desk and throw them through the window.

'That teacher was a full-on peddo with the things he used to do. And then he made me repeat and he did those things to me for another whole year.'

And I blasted the Rev's office like nobody's business.

The Rev said straight up, 'Clem, what you have just told me would make anybody very angry and I respect your rage. Is there any more you want to tell me?'

I was still blasting and I said, 'I reckon that teacher set me up against my dad and that was part of it, and he set me up with having to repeat and that was another part of it, and he did both those set-up tricks coz he wanted to do nasty things to me. And that teacher tracked me on my front wheel two whole years in a row.'

And that sounds like it is only a metaphor but it was like a bomb going off in me coz suddenly I knew what he had been doing in that set-up and I was radioactive about that.

The Rev waited for a while as the explosion cleared and he said, 'Clem is there anything else you want to say about this?' And that was it for me, to have someone listening like that, and that bomb blast in my head must have shaken some brain cells into action coz I stood there and I yelled out loud about how that teacher followed me in his mind.

That teacher was following me coz he could see I was feeling bad about not having a mum and I was feeling bad about how she died and he took a boy who was feeling bad and he made that boy actual bad until he was industrial strength dangerous on everyone and that boy was me.

'And another thing that teacher did,' I yelled at the Rev, 'was that he could see the boy's father was feeling bad and he made that father feel bad on the boy and that boy was his own son and it was me.

'And about that teacher I would like to have his head in one hand and a blunt instrument in the other hand but there aren't enough blunt instruments in this crappy world and that's the truth.'

I was fit to blister but I had not lost it on myself to cry coz I was so angry. And I said to the Rev, 'If I was a visual I could just close my eyes on all this but a kinesthetic can't do that and here I am.' And that was when I ran out of batteries.

The Rev was not slippery on this one and he said, 'Clem, we can do some specific things about what you have told me and I am prepared to do whatever it takes for the police to deal with that teacher.'

When he said that something in me let go. The first time in my life I ever felt like that. Relieved, afraid, all good. I don't know how we finished the session.

Clem.

DvD Review in 100 words
Clem Clams for the Coppers

We went for the interview at the
police station. I can't tell you
what happened as it is too much
shame for me. But I keep seeing it
in my mind like it's a DvD inside my
eyelids that won't shut down.
This time it is not black and white.

THURSDAY, SEPTEMBER 17
GOING TO THE COPPERS

Dear Gram

I will tell you about going to the police and I hope the DVD of it stops in my mind but this is hard and that is the truth. It was Dad and me at the police station and two policemen and a youth support officer. And it was very serious in there.

The first thing they asked was my name and birthday. They said I was there for a very serious interview about things that had been done to me and they asked me that teacher's name and that is when the terrible thing happened.

I tried to say that name but nothing happened except that my eyes turned to stones like Nick's that day.

Then instead of saying his name my stomach turned upside down and I got up and tried to run but it exploded all over the floor in front of me. And there was no warning and the spew went everywhere and even down my shirt.

But something else had happened and I could feel it and I just sort of crumpled over and hid behind the chair coz I have not messed in my pants like that since I was a baby and it was full-on shame to me. And Dad got down there beside me and held my shoulders together and

I could smell the sick and also the stinking mess that I made of my pants. And we sat like that for a long while.

Then the support worker told us that they had a bathroom with a shower and they could fix me up with some clean clothes. And she said that sometimes a person wants so bad to get rid of someone from his life that this happens.

So the interview finished without me saying anything and especially not that teacher's name and the support person took Dad and me for a milkshake. Dad told me that I had what it takes to get through this and I didn't come this far just to keep my shirt clean. That messed up interview is the DVD that keeps playing in my mind.

I am feeling not fully OK if the truth be told.

Love from Clem.

SATURDAY, SEPTEMBER 19
AWESOME WEEKEND

Dear Gram

Weekends get me feeling better and I am not thinking about police interviews today.

The Carters invited Dad and me to a BBQ. Violet had a present for me and it was a t-shirt but the writing was back to front.

'Put it on in front of the mirror,' she told me, so we went inside.

In the mirror that t-shirt said, 'You're awesome.' I stood there but had to keep blinking and I read it again.

'We all know it,' Violet said, 'but you have trouble believing it.' My eyes got misty and she hugged me until the others must be hungry by now.

Out at the BBQ Mr Carter said, 'There's prawns and veal kebabs and fancy sausages. What'll it be?'

'What are veal kebabs?' I said.

'Skewered steak,' he said, 'but from a baby calf and not a bullock.'

'I'll have prawns and sausages,' I said, coz I could only think about our calf at school. And I said, 'What's the song about Mr Bojangles?' And Violet's parents and Dad tried to sing it. Bad news, my dad singing.

Mr Bojangles is a dancer and he jumps so high and he lightly touched down and he had a little dog that died and I think the Rev set me up with that song.

But this is the weekend and I am out to enjoy.

From Clem the T-shirt Man. Awesome.

TUESDAY, SEPTEMBER 22
WHAT DO YOU DO WHEN TIME STANDS STILL?

Dear Gram

Another day another week another month. Sometimes that is how time feels and especially when things are running normal time, which is called chronology. But there are some days that have danger moments and then time stands still or it just disappears.

We had Values for Life class the other day with Mr German, and the values class had sentence number four in it that said, 'Silence or violence, are they the only two responses?' And we were very silent I can tell you coz we remembered that day of the message about Hamish and how this sentence was there on the board.

Mr German got us into thinking mode. He asked about how to respond to Bundy who sold Hamish the drugs, which is really hard coz Bundy was one of us. Well, that is when the chronology stopped. Hamish and Bundy were both at the school with us and then they were both gone.

I didn't know what to say about that sentence and that was wrong because it meant I was choosing the silence but that sentence only gives two choices and there are more than two, I know it.

The time of that class didn't follow the normal rules of chronology, like when the bike chain slips the sprockets and you go nowhere. Hamish was a demon on the trails and he deserves for me to be different about him than either silence or violence. But I don't know what.

It's like the hands of a clock. You look away then you look back and they've changed but you never see them moving. Time is standing still. It's waiting for me to make up my mind.

From timeless Clem.

Mr Hartley Gets Serious

Thought for the day: 'Life is about deciding whether you are going to stare up the steps or step up the stairs'.

It was funnier the day he said it like this, 'When I was sixteen I woke up and knew that I had to get through school or I had to start using my brain. So I made my choice and here I am.'

THURSDAY, SEPTEMBER 24
THE SWAP

Dear Gram

We had the second police interview, which is when I said how that teacher did a set-up on me and Dad and it was about my poster that I did for ecology.

The police asked me to tell them how it started.

I said, 'That teacher got us to do posters on ecology as homework and the best three posters would get trophies. He had those trophies sitting on his desk. But when we handed in the posters things had changed.'

He said, 'None of these posters is up to standard for first prize and so I am going to award only the second and third prizes.'

I got third prize, and I could tell that everyone was a bit upset that there were only two prizes. That afternoon the teacher kept me in. He said, 'Clem, I've thought about your poster and I think it's worth first prize after all. Are you happy about that?'

I said, 'Yes.'

Then he said, 'But the problem is that if I give you the first prize this late everybody else will get upset, especially the person who got second prize. We wouldn't want anybody to get upset, would we?'

'No,' I said.

'So you have a problem, don't you?'

'Yes.'

'So the way out of the problem is that you will have to take the trophy home with you and not have it on your desk. And it will have to be a secret. Does that sound like it will fix your problem?'

'Yes,' I said.

I sure liked having that first prize trophy. But I didn't like having that secret. The next afternoon he kept me there again. I had to sit in the classroom while he worked and everybody left. Then he started to ask me questions.

'Well, Clem, did you keep the secret of the trophy?'

'Yes.'

'You didn't tell anyone, did you?'

'No.'

'I have another secret for you to keep, a really important secret. Come with me.'

And he took me to the storeroom at the end of the school. He was breathing strange and he told me to stand still but when he began to take my clothes off I knew it was the end of me. And that afternoon in the storeroom made two secrets that I had to keep.

Those two secrets got to three and four and he would keep me in and do things to me and he was keeping me in over homework and posters.

But he never gave out prizes again.

Dad said to the police, 'We've got that poster at home, the one about ecology.'

'Are you sure it's the same one?' the police officer asked.

'Yes. There's only one on ecology. But there are others that I kept.'

'Clem,' one of them said, 'you said the teacher kept you in over homework and posters. Can you tell us more about that, please?'

I told them, 'If I handed in a poster the teacher would find a problem with it and keep me in. And when everybody else had gone from the school he would take me to the storeroom. I didn't even want to do posters any more.'

The police asked Dad if he had kept many posters from back then.

'I kept them all, until that teacher started to tell me what Clem's behaviour was like in school. Then I didn't want to keep them.'

Dad's eyes were not looking at anybody and he said, 'The teacher told me things about Clem and I believed him. He said Clem was always lying and couldn't be trusted by the teachers, and the other kids didn't like him. The teacher said Clem's behaviour should be expected because his mother had died. And I believed the teacher instead of Clem.'

Dad was holding his jaw tight and his eyes were in strife and it was trouble to me to see Dad like that and he couldn't even look at me but just spoke those words into the floor. Everyone was quiet and then Dad looked up at me and said, 'Clem, I am so sorry,' and his voice disappeared. The heat was making our faces distorted and distant, like at the campfire.

'Mr Dylan,' the policemen said, 'we'd like to see any posters that you have kept. They might give us a date for each offence.'

And then they said to me, 'Clem, the next interview might be pretty tough. When we have the posters and check for dates, we will need you to tell us all you can remember of what that man did to you each time. It is likely to be upsetting for you, but nobody here will embarrass you deliberately.' And I said, 'OK.'

And that was the second interview that was so terrible for Dad and me, but the police thought it was very positive because of those posters. I was scared of messing my daks again but I told them the teacher's name this time without the mess.

Clem.

WEDNESDAY, SEPTEMBER 30
GETTING MR BOJANGLES

Dear Gram

I went to see the Rev and faced him up straight.

'You set me up with that Bojangles song when we were talking about the calf and about Hamish being light on his feet.'

The Rev was up to it and said, 'Clem, I didn't mean to set you up and especially not to make you more upset about Hamish.'

There was no slippery sentences in there and I said, 'It wasn't about Hamish it was about my dad.'

'Perhaps you could tell me about your dad.'

'In that song where the little dog dies it says, 'after twenty years he still grieves.' That part of the song is like my dad still grieving my mum after all these years. I only just figured that out.'

'Clem, if you look closely you might see that you are also a bit like Mr Bojangles. But I didn't have that in mind when I spoke about the song.'

I had to screw my eyes shut when he said that but even my own eyes wouldn't help me. What the Rev said was the honest truth. And I said, 'For my whole life there is some part of the chronology that isn't working and is standing still and I don't know how to get it running. But this year lots of things have started up for me.'

We waited for me to get OK, and the Rev said, 'Lots of people record the Bojangles song, but my favourite is by a guy named Bob Dylan.'

'One day you might get to hear a song by Clem Dylan.'

'That would be OK by me,' he said.

So that is my week or month or was it just a day I don't know. Just as well we've got holidays coming up. I need some time out from all this while the clock catches up.

With love from Clem who is starting to love himself.

FRIDAY, OCTOBER 2
INTERVIEW THREE

Dear Gram

The third police interview is over. Dad had all my posters from home and the police asked me to tell them about any that I could remember when the teacher had done stuff to me, except they were now calling it sexual assault.

And there were more posters than I could remember about and there were dates on those posters. There were some posters that didn't have bad memories for me. But lots of other times he did stuff to me and I did not have the posters or know the dates.

I started out OK but when we got to the stuff in the storeroom I lost it right there in the police station.

'That man took off all my clothes and he started doing things to me with his hands and then with his mouth,' and by then I was charging round that interview room like I used to in session. 'And it went to even worse from there coz it got to where he would take his own clothes off and on those days I knew it was going to be very dangerous for me.'

I reckon those coppers must have been taking lessons from the Rev coz they just sat there and listened and took notes and that whole interview was being recorded and they got me on record charging round that room fit to take somebody's head off his shoulders. I was radioactive, but I knew I could meet the challenge on this one and I had what it takes.

It took a bit of charging around before I got calm enough to go through those posters and tell the police everything I could remember about what he did without going right off. Eventually I got to the end. But the difference this time was that I hadn't run out of batteries.

And those police had to take full–on crap

from me before we got all those memories out.

Then the surprise happened. The police told us that this teacher was already in prison for doing sexual assault on other kids. There were several people who charged him who were now adults and I was the youngest boy to talk with the police. And nearly every person had the story of the third prize trophy.

That man was doing the same stuff to kids for years before I was in his class and I really got mad and was back up and yelling things about that man and what should happen to him for doing terrible things to so many little kids. And everyone sat and listened as I shouted until this time I did run out of batteries. When I sat down again Dad and me just looked at each other.

The police told us that he had been in prison for over a year and he would be there for another eight years but he would be formally charged over what he did to me and he would be there for even longer. It was a very quiet finish to the interview that day and the support person took Dad and me off for a smoothie so we could slow down.

And so that's the interviews finished Gram, and they were pure toxic on me but all that teacher's set-up on Dad and me is now over.

Clem.

Clem's Song - verse 1

Don't know where I've been,

Or the life that I've been making.

It wasn't coz of giving,

But of someone else's taking.

Got lost along the way.

A path of litter lying,

Through piled up dust of years,

The dried up dust of dying.

WEDNESDAY, OCTOBER 21
KEVLAR & CHRONOLOGY &
CRYING CLEM CLEAN

Dear Gram

Holidays were top stuff, but I didn't spend much time out on the track this time. Most of it riding around town or with Violet or with thinking about writing this song.

We're back to school and Wednesday is my normal session day.

I told the Rev about the police interviews and he listened like he usually does and that means that something's coming and I had better watch out. He only said, 'I wonder why that teacher picked you and not some other boy.' That sounded safe enough and I was relaxed a bit after the holidays. Not smart, that relaxing. Suddenly I knew what that teacher had done and I wasn't so safe after all.

'He was using Kevlar protection!' I yelled. I jumped up and bounced the palms of my hands against the window. I wanted it to break, but was glad it didn't. I turned around to look at the Rev. 'I was already hurting and the teacher chose me so he could hold up my hurt to protect himself. And whenever I started to go off about that teacher he would say I was still hurting over my mum and everyone believed him and not me.'

'I think you've got it,' said the Rev.

Something changed when he said that. Everything outside went quiet. I could feel my heart beating inside my chest. My eyes started to give me up and I crumpled into a chair while the whole universe slowed down. I sat like that for ages. Eventually I said to the Rev, 'Can you say a prayer for me?'

And he said OK and didn't even close his eyes.

'Hey God . . .' he said, which was so disrespectful and I looked at him shocked and was going to say something but he said, 'Hey God, where do you want to be working in Clem's life?'

His prayer was over and the chronology stopped and I found out how risky it is to be a kinesthetic.

I was in a flashback up above the trees and looking down at a tree house and a boy who should have been at a funeral except he was waiting for a door to open.

This time I knew what I had been thinking up there in that war zone of a tree house when Dad came to get me.

A dangerous feeling crept up inside me and it was this thing called grief which is about sadness and loss, but is also about being angry and it's about terrible fear. That dangerous feeling was very scary for me.

The grief with its anger and its fear must have been sleeping pretty lightly coz it came awake easy when the Rev said that prayer.

The tree house dissolved and I was standing in the same backyard, a lonely little boy who wanted a mum but there wasn't one for him. And I could see myself crying there in the backyard. Then the grief hit me and my crying really started.

Not crying like has happened before in session, but crying from waaay waaay back that went on as if it was never going to end. Crying like a flood that breaks the banks of a river and spreads out over the country. This crying was like being in the path of a flooding river.

The river started washing things along with it. The crying was washing away those old lonely feelings. My life was full of empty places where memories should have been and it had this hollow sound of longing and loneliness and the flood took it all and cleared it out. And it went on until I got washed out to sea and was floating there in peace at last.

I don't know how I survived that flood of grief it was so strong and that is the honest truth. Don't even know how long I was crying. Never cried so much or so long and it was about my mum who I never met.

The crying steadied up and the flood drained

away but the floating out to sea stayed for a while and I was on the floor and couldn't stand up for a long time. When I could move again I was aching all over. The Rev was looking at what was happening and he was OK to just let it happen until I could get into a chair again.

That prayer by the Rev came straight from outer space and that is how I got to be cleaned up by that river and that is the amazing truth and I am still a bit weird about that crying, and more than a bit I can tell you.

I like the way it has left me and I don't have to blame myself for my mum dying any more. And it all came about coz I thought I was safe but the Rev asked that shocker of a question about 'Why me?'

I lost an hour of my life in that flood on the Rev's floor but the chronology has started up again and there's a new life coming.

Love,

Clem.

Clem's Song - verse 2 & Chorus

It's peaceful in the dark
Coz then the world is safer.
That locked in state of mind
Keeps trembling terrors calmer.

But when the river came
It washed away the grieving,
It took the secret shame,
It flooded me with mercy.

Coming down, coming near,
Coming soon, coming home.
Coming in, coming close,
Coming now, coming home.

SATURDAY, OCTOBER 24
MEGA-APOLOGELATO – HA HA`

Dear Gram

I feel like I've been knocking forever on some door trying to get into my own life. But when the door finally opened I found that I'd been knocking from the inside. The world's a different place.

There's a birthday on my mind which is coming closer every minute. Yeehar! Dad gave me my bike even before my birthday and now he's planning something else.

'Can you handle a little surprise in a few days?' he said and I said, 'OK,' with a big grin. It's getting like I need wider cheek bones.

Got home from school on Friday arvo and Dad and I have been looking at each other and grinning ever since. It's as if we both know what's coming up but not telling. Well, I don't know what, but something sure is cooking, I can tell by his eyes.

I am burning up inside about this birthday and the Screamin' Demon is waiting as much as I am. That bike has a happy heart. We both only have to wait until tomorrow.

Violet and her mum and dad came for a BBQ today. I had a rubber chicken sitting there and I gave it to Mr Carter. 'You can do the cooking,'

I told him. Violet started giggling and I could tell her mum was trying hard to hold it in as well.

Mr Carter said with a big grin, 'It looks like we are all going hungry.'

I said, 'I am mega apologelato about that,' and grinned back.

'Mega what?' he asked.

'I am mega apologelato, which is Italian for being so sorry that I will buy everyone an ice-cream.'

Well, Violet got the giggles so bad she couldn't stop. Violet laughs like a waterfall in the mountains and I just want to dive right in. I love that.

We got the cooking done and Dad and me were being fully funny talking with each other across the table.

Dad said, 'I've been thinking. Clem. Thought I'd get myself another bike so we could go riding together. What do you reckon? Been a long time since I had a bike.'

'That'd be good.' I added, 'Think you could handle the track at school?'

'Easy.'

'What about down the gully?'

'A mate of mine is the gully-master. I'll get him to teach me.'

'That means you'll have a better teacher than I did.'

Violet was giggling again and I nearly cracked up.

'I'll have to get proper riding shirt and pants. That sound OK to you, Clem? I'm not too old for proper riding gear am I?'

'What if I help you with the shopping? You can pay me commission.'

'What about a crash hat? I like the one Ned Kelly used to wear.'

'With a head like that you need a crash hat?'

And we were talking like that with each other and with Mr and Mrs Carter laughing along with us and Violet giggling all the way. Dad and I had the funnest time ever.

But tomorrow is the day.

Love from Clem.

Clem's Song – Verse 3

The world's a different place
And the difference is inside me.
The locked door of my life
Is full-on off its hinges.
The toxic fear is gone,
That's the straight-up truth
   I tell you.

Now a boy with half a life
Can have a proper future.

Coming down, coming near,
Coming soon, coming home.
Coming in, coming close,
Coming now, coming home.

A NEW DAY

Dear Mum

It's October 25th, and we know what that means.

'Happy birthday, dear Clem.' You would want to say that to me, I know it. It's been a long time coming, but I was born for days like this.

Got up early coz I didn't want to miss anything today. Dad was getting breakfast already. How did he manage to cook up a bunch of toast without waking me up? You sure picked a special bloke, and am I glad.

He said, 'Happy Birthday, Clem,' and we gave each other a big hug. That's not the usual but we both just did it. Felt good, too, and I couldn't help but think of you.

I thought he might say something about buying his new bike so we could go riding together, but he pulled out a big parcel instead.

That parcel was heavy and gnarly and there was no telling what was in there. But inside were pants like Robocop and a tag with Dad's work logo on it. They were thick and industrial and definitely not mountain bike pants and inside those pants there was this yellow layer of Kevlar protection.

I said to Dad, 'These are funny bike pants,' and he said, 'Here is the next parcel.'

And inside the next parcel, which was just as lumpy through the paper, there was this jacket and I could see straight off that it was a wicked motorbike jacket and it had his logo on the sleeve and I looked at Dad and he said, 'Come and see my new toy.'

Dad stood up and I had to hurry to catch him up. He went quick to the shed and turned on the light and there was this madaz Aprilia Pegaso 650 Trail. There were two helmets there on the seat and he gave me one that had Ned Kelly painted on it and said, 'This helmet is for you, Clem. Happy birthday.'

I was standing there in shock and Dad's eyes were sparkly out there in the shed and he said, 'There's a pillion seat and room for a passenger and I will be full-on careful with you on the back.'

And that is the honest truth fully straight-up I can tell you.

*The correct lyrics to
'The Times They Are A-Changin' ' are:

> *Come mothers and fathers throughout the land
> And don't criticise what you can't understand
> Your sons and your daughters are beyond your
> command*

The 'Questions They Ask When We Stuff Up' comes from the Restorative Justice work of Terry O'Connell of Real Justice Australia. Terry was instrumental in the formation of young offender community conferencing in Australia. The questions are quoted with his permission. He also advised me on Police procedures for other parts of the book. Terry's work can be followed up at RealJustice.org

ACKNOWLEDGMENTS

Firstly I want to thank Clem. One night this book started to write itself in my head and that is where I met Clem. If I got a bit off line with the story Clem was always there to set me straight and he is fully cool for doing that for me.

To my younger friend, Zoe Littlejohns, who taught me a bit of texting. Zoe is a brand new schoolteacher and she will full on love those kids and I want to be in her class and Zoe appears in this book.

To my older friend Lewis Elliott who was known to school kids as the BFG. Lewis saw me writing this book and offered two lines to inspire me. Those lines became sentences one and two on the sad day of Hamish. His words had extra meaning when I heard of his illness. Lewis died, 87 years young, just before this book came to print.

To my friends Piers and Margaret Hartley from Bogong Outdoor Education Centre where piers was Principal. There's a generation of school kids who have enjoyed their unique blend of mad humour, wisdom, and deep humanity, and who will recognise them in this book.

To two friends in the literary world, John Cohen of *Reading Time*, and Tessa Wooldridge of Austlit, who gave me encouragement and advice through the early editing stage. They gave momentum to my own faltering efforts.

A special thank you to children's author, Hazel Edwards. I met Hazel at a writers' conference where she read a draft of this book. She could see the real Clem in among my messy writing, and she took his story very seriously. Hazel's mentoring and assistance has been the springboard from which Clem's story comes to print.

Mostly I want to thank my wife Kay who sat around without me while I wrote this book on a camping holiday. Clem has been a guest in our house for three years. Now he's gone into the world on his own two feet and we can have another go at that holiday.

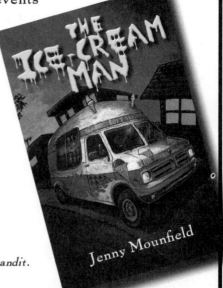